ANGEL RISES

SOUL FORGE BOOK TWO

LESLIE CLAIRE WALKER

**My name is Night Sanchez. Every choice I make is a second chance
to fight for love...**

iii

I've saved my kid and found family from the ghosts that haunt me.
I've found a tempting love willing to stand by the new me, the good
person I'm working so hard to become. Our power, skill, and courage
bought us time. But will it be enough?

The Order hasn't forgotten my betrayal. They'll keep sending
assassins. I'm smarter, faster, and stronger than any of them—so far.

The Angel of Death strains at the chains that bind him, threatening
to break my mind. He struggles for freedom, but my magic holds tight
—so far.

A new power storms the gates. One who forces me to take my
family on the run. To stay one step ahead—until now.

Enemies on all sides? That's a perfect storm. Luck can only hold
out for so long. And the worst part? My people assemble like super-
heroes. They won't let me fight this battle alone. That means I can't
keep them safe. Not this time.

We triumph together, or we fall...

ALSO BY LESLIE CLAIRE WALKER

THE AWAKENED MAGIC SAGA

THE SOUL FORGE

(The Complete Series)

Angel Hunts

Angel Rises

Angel Falls

Angel Strikes

Angel Roars

Angel Burns

THE FAERY CHRONICLES

(The Complete Series)

Faery Novice

Faery Prophet

Faery Sovereign

SHORT STORY COLLECTIONS

Ink & Blood

Ink & Stars

Ink & Sword

CHAPTER 1

I OPENED MY eyes wide, fisting my hands in the down comforter on my bed. The rush of my own blood roared in my ears, my heart racing. The textured white ceiling above rocked back and forth for an uncanny moment before it stilled.

The warmth of the bed made it clear that the recurring nightmare had released me. I was no longer at the bottom of the churning river, struggling to reach the surface, but home, in the here and now. The ribbed black tank I'd worn to bed hugged my curves. The edge of my panties had ridden up my right cheek during the night.

Dust motes floated in the air, backlit by the morning light that streamed in through the wooden slats of the window blinds. The sage-green walls looked soft and welcoming. On the wall opposite the bed, the burnished bronze frame and mirror glowed. The scent of baked potatoes and barbecue beef—last night's dinner—perfumed the air.

Yep, home.

The sounds inside my head subsided, leaving the patter of December rain on the glass and the deep, steady breathing of my lover, Red.

Breathing deep, but not asleep.

He whispered in my ear, his voice gravelly, with a touch of East Texas. "Another one, Night?"

"Same one," I said. "Third time this week."

He raised up on one elbow and leaned close. His halo—the field of life force around his body—shone grass green and earth brown. He even smelled like grass and earth. Steady. Strong. It was a reflection of his magic, so different from my own.

He studied me with sharp green eyes, their corners crinkled with concern. His white skin still held onto the barest kiss of the summer sun. Shaggy, salt-and-pepper hair framed his face, with a shaggy mustache to match.

His hair had started to turn at the age of sixteen. He'd had a shock to the system. The shock had been me.

He'd lived next door to my family in Houston, and witnessed the aftermath of what happened the night my parents were killed. He'd taken me in—a brown girl splattered with blood and stinking of smoke. He'd hidden me, saved my life, and lost me, all within the course of a single day twenty years ago.

I'd been twelve years old, scared and alone and wounded to the depths of my soul. The Order of the Blood Moon, a secret organization of magical assassins, had plucked me from the street where I lived and taken me in. They'd trained me to use my magic for their ends. I'd become one of them. They were my family. My home.

All that changed the night they'd sent me to kill a family.

No one had left the Order and lived to tell about it—until me. The magical assassins demanded that its operatives obey or die, but I'd broken free, and the Order had been hunting me ever since. I never wanted to place another person in the Order's sights.

Unbelievably, Red had volunteered.

That we'd found each other again couldn't have been an accident— it had to have been fate.

I'd arrived in Portland, Oregon, on the run, with my daughter, Faith, in tow. I'd applied for a job at Justice Gym, which he owned, and he'd given it to me, no questions asked. It wasn't that he'd recognized me—I'd changed too much. But he'd used his magic to read me, and whatever he'd seen had been enough to allow for trust. Afterward, when danger had rained down in the form of the Angel of Death, he offered his help. All the while, too, he'd offered the promise of his love.

I was still trying to figure out what that meant. Opening my heart meant a kind of vulnerability that I'd never been very good at. Loving me also made the person I cared for a target.

"What's the dream?" he asked. "Which test?"

It was always a test. I was always terrified I'd fail, that I'd never be good enough. That I'd never be enough.

I took a deep breath and blew it out slow and steady. That simple act took my nerves down several notches. "Water survival during my early training with the Order. I nearly drowned. Sunday and I made it. Our friend Miguel didn't. We were thirteen."

Red didn't press for more details, for which I felt profoundly grateful. I could still taste muddy water and electric fear, and I didn't want to dive back in. What he did say made me want to pummel him with my pillow.

"What else?" he asked.

"What makes you think there's something else?"

He raised a brow.

"What?" I asked.

"I know you," he said. "Besides, I see it in you."

That was his magic, untainted and untrained. He'd had it from birth, and unlike my gift, it had always belonged to him and him alone.

Red saw into people by gazing into them, marking who and what they were. He could tell good from bad, and truth from lies. He could see the spark of potential—all the possibilities in a person's path. He used his magic to build people up, to convince people of their shine.

And to call them on their bullshit.

"The ghost of my memory," I said. "The one I repressed the night my parents died."

His brow furrowed. "I remember."

"It was a warning," I said. "The ghost said, *He's not what he seems.*"

He narrowed his eyes. "Nothing ominous about that."

I sighed.

The "he" in the warning was the Angel of Death, the one from the Book of Revelations. He'd shown up a month ago, real as—well, death. *La Muerte.* He'd arrived in search of a human body, a vessel, in which to walk the world. He had a job to do, what with kicking off the Apocalypse, and the time had come. I had the juice to carry him.

He'd gone after me with everything he had, intending to subjugate my mind to his will. His plan had backfired spectacularly. I carried him inside my mind now, sleeping and waking—at every moment.

I didn't know how long I could hold him, only that it couldn't be forever. And I sure didn't want to know that the Angel of Death was not what he seemed. Not without a more detailed explanation.

"You feelin' all right?" Red asked.

I met his gaze. "Aside from the nightmare? Yeah."

"No strange sensations? No hallucinations? No signs that the Angel in your mind is breaking free?"

I bit my lip. "You know I'm worried about that."

"That's not what I'm asking," he said.

"I know," I said. "No. No signs that I can tell. Everything feels the same as it has since that night. Like he's locked up tight."

Red mulled that a moment. "You want me to wake you next time?"

"No."

"You sound sure about that."

I felt sure. "If there are messages coming through, then I need to hear them."

"Or memories," he said. "More things floating to the surface."

I'd had only the one repressed memory in my life, not a dozen. I opened my mouth to say so, then closed it. There were plenty of things about my life before the Order that I didn't remember. Things about my parents and the rest of my family. The Order had taken my culture and given me theirs. The missions I'd undertaken had destroyed me further. Who knew what else I might be missing?

My mind was a wonder of magic and power. It was also a goddamn mystery—one I needed to understand.

"Promise you'll let whatever happens in my dreams play out," I said.

"Cross my heart." He leaned closer, holding my gaze.

I poked him in the chest, my fingertip running up against a streak of silver hair and a whole lot of muscle. "How do I know I'm not still dreaming? How do I know you're not a hallucination?"

His lips curved. "You want me to prove I'm real?"

I lifted my head to kiss him. He met me halfway, reaching with his free hand to cradle my head.

I closed my eyes, breathing him in as his lips moved gently over mine, the fall of his hair shading my face from the morning light. For a moment, the brush of his mustache along my lip and the sandpaper roughness of the shadow on his cheeks and the salt taste of him became my whole world. When I looked at him again, the spark in his eyes ignited a fire inside of me.

He saw it before he felt it. I read that on his face, in a flash of wonder that he tucked away almost as soon as it surfaced.

He lowered my head to the pillow again, tracing a finger along the line of my cheek, then down my arm, stopping to trace the lines of my scars. The souvenir from a knife fight, white against my light brown skin. The half-moon below my elbow, darker and much older. I didn't even know how I'd ended up with that one.

"How much time have we got?" he asked.

I didn't need to check the electronics to answer, not with the quality of the light. "Not enough."

He sighed. "I'll get the coffee started."

I nodded.

He planted a kiss between my eyebrows, then rolled out of bed, reaching for the faded jeans he'd tossed onto the floor last night. He stood tall and pulled them on over his beautiful, boxer-clad butt.

I felt a twinge of regret, not being able to appreciate him properly, but duty called. I slid out from under the comforter, the chill in the air turning the skin of my bare arms and legs to gooseflesh. An icy feeling, a flash from the nightmare, settled over me again.

Red glanced over his shoulder at me. He saw what I felt. He didn't say anything. He just made his way out of the room, zipping his jeans along the way. His footfalls echoed across the bamboo floor of the skinny hall that led to the kitchen. From down that way, I heard the door to the freezer open and shut. He'd grabbed the coffee, as promised. Then in the usual succession, the sluice of water from the kitchen faucet filling the kettle. The soft clang of the kettle being set on an electric burner. Sudden heat sizzling stray drops from the kettle's bottom.

Some things, we couldn't do anything about. The nightmares I had. The sense of foreboding. Those things were born from my experiences, my fears. Unless—or until—they manifested, they were only ghosts. If the Angel of Death was responsible for them rising in me? Nothing to do but keep an eye on it.

The one thing we could actually deal with—whatever lay between us—we didn't talk about, as if by unspoken agreement. We spent time together. We slept together. We blew off steam. We played. There was more to it than that, but we tried not to take it deeper. To invest more felt like a greater risk than either of us was prepared to take right now, in the breath before the storm descended.

Our shared history complicated things. Beyond that, my past presented a serious obstacle. It wasn't as if I'd just been a normal person who'd made some bad decisions. I'd been an assassin. There was so much blood on my hands, I could drown in it.

So Red and I engaged with each other as best we could, and if both of us kept defenses up to guard the tender places in our hearts, neither of us intended to breach them. Not yet.

I sighed. Then I pulled on my own jeans and curled my toes in the pile of the champagne carpet. I squared my shoulders and pushed away dread and worry. Holding on to it wouldn't do any good. Better to eat and caffeinate and take a look at it wide awake. Develop a strategy. Make plans. Carry them out. Thought and action versus fear. Fear could not be allowed to win.

That was who I was. What I did.

I padded into the hall, casting a glance to the right, toward the darkened bedroom next door where my daughter usually slept. She'd spent last night with friends—a good thing for her, even if it seemed strange after so long on the run to let her go her own way. Faith was a teenager, and staying over with friends was what teenagers did.

We had as many things to worry about as we did before the Angel showed up on our doorstep. Back then, the Order chased us from one place to the next. Faith and I spent years finding new hideouts, creating new identities, looking over our shoulders. Our vigilance kept us alive.

When we'd arrived in Portland, something shifted. We'd found people we cared about. We'd made a start at a real home. The Angel of Death coming after us changed things, too. We might be able to outrun the Order, but the Angel? How could anyone hide from a being like that? So, we'd agreed to make a stand.

I worried about Faith when she was away from me, but I couldn't keep her by my side twenty-four seven. She and her group of friends all had their fair share of magic, and they had each other. They knew to ask for help if and when they needed it. That was all I could hope for.

The doorbell rang, a huge, startling sound that gonged through the apartment—Faith's way of breaking up whatever shenanigans Red and I might be up to before she used her key. She'd caught us kissing once and had turned several shades of red.

She'd pointed out to me that Red had feelings for me before I'd seen it. She'd seemed cool with it. She'd said as much. But no way did she ever want to accidentally run into us doing something worse—her words, not mine.

I was, for all intents and purposes, still her mother.

She turned her key in the lock and wrapped her hand around the doorknob. No alarm sounded. The only magical people allowed to enter the apartment were those with a standing invitation. The spell laid into the knob would shock any other magic user hard enough to knock them out.

My family and I were here to stay in Portland. That was no excuse to be careless.

The door swung open on creaking hinges, flooding the entry with light, highlighting the thin layer of dust that overlay the small, teak-wood table and the hall tree that hung above it, half of its silver hooks and peacock-feather paint job hidden by Red's and my coats and scarves.

The light streamed far enough to illuminate the living room. TV tucked into the corner. A painting of Our Lady of Guadalupe, starry-cloaked and crowned in fiery gold, hung over the white-painted brick of the fireplace. Outdoor snowflake lights, strung across the mouth of the hearth, glowed Christmas colors. A scarred oak coffee table held down a denim-blue rug. Beat-up denim sofa. Scratched and dinged black dining table pushed against the wall closest to me.

Faith took a careful step inside. She met my gaze with soft brown eyes. Her voice had a foggy, stayed-up-half-the-night ring to it. "Y'all decent?"

I rolled my eyes.

She shook her head. "That's my silent line you're stealing, Night."

"Yeah, yeah," I said.

Her halo shimmered its usual deep silver, though this morning its edges tended toward a somber gray. She dropped her backpack on the floor, toed off a pair of black hiking boots that she hadn't bothered to lace in the first place, and unzipped her silver down parka, shrugging it off and hanging it on a free hook on the hall tree above the table.

Her ruby-red V-neck sweater and black jeans looked like they'd gone ten rounds with her friend Corey's white kitty. Faith had managed a shower, and she still smelled like pinion-scented shampoo and soap. The ends of her long, dark, waves were curled and damp. A closer look showed a set of lightweight luggage under her eyes. The corners of her mouth turned down. Not enough to make a frown, mind, but definitely enough to telegraph that she had something she didn't want to tell me.

"Y'all have fun last night?" I asked.

She dropped keys on the entry table. They landed with a musical *clink*. "We did divination."

Fortunetelling. "About what?"

"Everything," she said.

"And?"

"You're gonna need coffee first."

On cue, the kettle on the stove began to whistle. Red lifted it off the heat. He'd heard every word, of course.

"Five minutes," he said. "Or is the world gonna end any earlier?"

Faith cleared her throat. "Morning to you, too, Red."

He chuckled.

Their easy friendship gave me hope. When I looked at them together, I saw a future I wanted for all of us, but it was one I felt afraid to dream. We might make it, but we wouldn't get out from under unscathed.

Where the Order was concerned, no one ever did.

I'd been the Order's number-two assassin for years, sneaking into the homes of targets, invading minds with my magic, using my power to take out the targets I'd been assigned. I'd had a one-hundred-percent follow-through rate on all of my missions, except the last one.

The Order had assigned me a family. Mother, father, kid. I'd murdered the female target in her sleep. Her husband hadn't been so lucky. He'd awakened before I could slip into his mind and take him peacefully, so he got a bullet for his trouble. The child had been the problem.

The child had been Faith.

She'd been like me when I was small. Her parents hadn't under-stood her gift. They'd hurt her. Locked her away. They'd tried to make her normal and, when they'd failed, they hid her. God only knew what they might've tried next.

I couldn't take her life myself, and I couldn't leave her there for the follow-up team to come along and finish the job. That left only one choice. I slipped away in the night, leaving the Order behind, taking Faith with me.

For the longest time, she hadn't known the circumstances under which I'd "adopted" her. She'd chosen to believe that I'd saved her from the Order operative who'd been sent to kill her. I'd shattered that belief, that innocence, a month ago because I'd had no choice. Now that Faith knew the truth, she'd accepted it as much as she could.

Some days, she blamed me. Other days, she clung to me. I was all she had, and she knew I felt the same.

We needed each other.

I pulled out a chair from the dinette. I pointed at Faith, then at the seat.

She hesitated. "There's a man coming."

"Another Order operative?" I asked.

"Yes," she said.

We'd expected this. The Order had tracked us here. They'd sent assassins after us. We'd taken them out. They'd send more.

"Just the one?" Red asked.

Faith nodded. "It's who he is that's the problem. Him. His magic."

Red sipped his coffee. "The man's magic is the problem? Or he's the problem, himself?"

"Both," Faith said. "It wasn't just the cards that said so. I also got messages while I was reading. You know, from..."

She trailed off.

I'd been in the process of lifting my mug to take the first sip. I lowered it slowly, and couldn't help notice that my hand trembled slightly as I did. I finished her sentence in my silent voice.

The Awakened.

Faith's magic had a source unlike any other I'd ever heard of before —a god that was a part of her soul. No one knew much about this god other than that it was very old and that it slept inside the soul of a human being, passed down through the generations via reincarnation. It would wake from its slumber at some point. No one knew when. What it might do afterwards was a mystery as well—one that even the Angel of Death seemed to fear.

If Faith was receiving messages from the sleeping god while doing a routine divination reading—that meant trouble, any way we sliced it. I wouldn't tell her it was all right, or act as if it was somehow normal or expected. After the business of withholding how she'd come to be with me, I wouldn't lie to her again.

I reached across the table and covered her hand with mine. She seemed to breathe a little deeper. Sit a little easier. I needed to be steady for her. If I was going to freak out, I'd have to do it on the inside.

Red set his cup down on the table and leaned back in his chair, folding his arms across his chest. "Did you read any clues in the cards about what this Order operative wants?"

Faith pulled her hand from beneath mine. "What do they always want?"

Red simply looked at her.

Faith stared right back at him.

Across the room, the front door opened unexpectedly on its noisy hinges. Only one other person had a key to the apartment, not that she'd had to use it this time.

Red cocked his head at Faith. "You don't lock the door behind you now?"

Faith's eyes widened. Red's tone hadn't been angry. He'd been teasing her. Teasing. At a time like this. "Are you made of steel or something?"

Sunday Sloan did what Faith had forgotten to—flip the deadbolt home behind her—and stepped inside the small, stuffed entry. The music of her voice preceded her, like the sound water made as it flowed over rocks. "Never let him fool you, Faith. He's made of feelings. Great big, mushy feelings."

"That's me," Red said. "Pile of mush."

Sunday shrugged out of her black trench coat, hanging it on top of mine. She peeled off a pair of gray wool gloves, tossing them on top of the keys. Thick blond curls brushed her shoulders. She wore the usual makeup on her porcelain face—just a pale pink flush of lipstick— along with a black T-shirt, black jeans, and steel-toe black boots with rubber soles. Practical.

Sunday had been my friend since I'd met her, and more beginning not long after the night of the survival test, when Miguel had drowned in the river. She'd been my lover. My soulmate. My salvation.

When I'd left the Order, I'd left her behind, too. She'd still believed in the Order. She was the best assassin they'd ever trained, and she had a thirst for killing. I wasn't altogether sure that she'd lost that thirst.

That made me wary, even if I understood it. I'd been the same, once upon a time. I'd figured the Order had sent me after targets for a good reason, that they deserved what they got. Simple lies that masked the complex truth—that the Order contracted to kill good people as well as bad.

I tried not to think about my targets—my victims. Recriminations served no purpose. That left me with atonement. How to balance the scales? I had to believe it could be done.

"What's the emergency?" Sunday asked.

I looked at Faith. "You called her?"

Faith flashed me her best dead-on *duh* expression. "All hands on deck."

Red answered Sunday's question. "Order operative on the way. Troublesome magic. Faith's sleeping god thinks it's a problem."

She hesitated on her way to the table, so briefly that anyone who didn't know her well probably wouldn't have picked up on it. "ETA?"

He raised his cup to her. "God only knows."

"Got any whisky to put in that coffee?" Sunday slipped past us, headed for the kitchen to grab another mug.

"Bourbon," Red said. "Cabinet to the left of the sink, bottom shelf."

Sunday returned with a mug, but no alcohol. She poured herself half of what remained in the press, offering the rest to me. When I shook my head, she topped off her portion.

"Changed your mind about the day drinking?" Red asked.

"You understand metaphors, right?" Sunday lifted her cup from the bottom and took a gulp rather than a sip.

"We're screwed?" Red asked.

"Like a porn star," Sunday said.

Faith's jaw dropped, and I stared at Sunday.

"What?" Sunday took another swig of coffee. She glanced at Faith. "Did your god say anything specific?"

Faith closed her mouth. After a moment, she said, "Purple."

"Purple what?" Sunday asked.

"That's it," Faith said. "Just the color."

Sunday leaned back in her chair. "I don't like the sound of that."

"What's it sound like?" Red asked.

"Like a chameleon," she said. "They're the only magicians who have purple halos."

I'd never met a chameleon. I'd only heard about them. Supposedly, their magic could camouflage them under any circumstances, like the creatures they'd been named after. They could also impersonate other people, down to the visible pores on a nose, down to the way a person smelled and tasted. They were uncanny, and the Order only brought them out when need dictated.

Chameleons were great at observation. Infiltration. They were sent in when the target was so important and so dangerous, failure was not an option.

"I was trained in how to spot one, so I should be able to," Sunday said. "Theoretically."

I downed the contents of my cup. "Wait—what? Why'd the Order train you for that, but not me?"

"I was part of a pilot program," she said. "The mentors were testing to see whether it was possible for someone who wasn't a chameleon to spot one—particularly someone who couldn't see magic the way you do, Night. Or you, Red. Soul-blind, they called it. They said it was because the chameleons would be needed on future missions, and the rest of us had to find a way to be able to work with them."

"They *said*?" I asked.

"I got the impression they were lying," Sunday said. "I got the impression they were afraid."

I whistled. If something—someone—had made the higher-ups at the Order nervous enough to show, we should be afraid, too.

"The first and only clue is the halo," she said. "It's purple, and it's not fixed. Also, their souls remain their own at the deepest level. That was what I was told. For the soul-blind, there's a shimmer that you can sometimes catch from the corner of your eye when the chameleon moves."

Red set down his cup. "That's it?"

Sunday nodded.

"Damn," he said.

I sat back. "How successful were you, spotting chameleons for the Order?"

"One out of twenty," she said.

Bad odds. "You get a sense of how many chameleons there are?"

She met my gaze. "They didn't tell me, but if I were guessing, I'd put the number at about a hundred."

"How could there be that many?" Red asked. "I mean, are there a shit ton of assassins who can blind their enemies with a single glance?"

"Just me," Sunday said. "Just like there's only one Night."

"Illustrates my point."

She sighed. "There's a thing that happens—a phenomenon, the mentors would call it—where when there's need in the world for a certain type of magic, it appears. More children who carry that kind of power are born to answer the need. According to the mentor I asked, that started happening with chameleons about twenty, thirty years ago. That's what I know."

"That's all?" Red asked.

"Unfortunately, yes." She looked at Red. "You need to take a look at all of us now, and you can start with me. Don't just look at the way my soul manifests. Don't just check my thoughts and feelings. Look deeper."

"This is practice?" he asked.

"You can think of it that way, sure," she said.

"And we need a baseline check to make sure that everyone in this room is who they say they are," he said.

She nodded.

"You're you," he said.

Faith blinked. "That fast? You already checked her?"

He nodded. It was what he did.

Faith pushed away from the table, rising to pace the length of the room, table to fireplace and back again. The rhythm of her steps grated. The tension in her body seemed too much for one girl to hold.

Sunday narrowed her eyes. "Anxious?"

"Aren't you?" Faith asked.

Sunday turned away without answering. "Night, you'll have to check Red. Can you do that?"

I nodded, then took a deep breath and focused my power on Red—on his grass and earth halo, the way it played on the edges of his skin. The warmth that radiated from him.

I slipped into his mind. My magic melded with his thoughts and emotions as if they were my own.

He trained his whole self—his perceptions and sensations—on me. I saw my face the way he did, through his eyes, noting the fall of my hair along the curve of my neck, the particular shade of brown that suffused my skin, the bow of my mouth. Pressure filled his chest—an overflow of feeling. Some of it was fear for what might happen. Most of it was love.

The depth of the emotion surprised me. I tried not to let that show.

I turned to his memories, rifling through them in search of the one I wanted, filled with darkness, and only a sliver of light creeping in through the crack between the double doors. The light flashed red and blue, red and blue. It came from the trucks outside on the street.

The hardwood floor of the closet hit every pressure point on Red's body. He couldn't lie still, which meant he couldn't sleep. Hell, he was a pure fool, as his mom would say, for even trying. The house next door had burned near to the ground. The fire department's best and brightest had done what they could to save it and the folks inside, but they'd been too late.

The lone survivor of the fire was a secret, and she was in his closet, out like a light and having dreams filled with terror, judging by the way she shook. She reeked of smoke and singed hair and other things he didn't want to imagine but couldn't help—melting plastic and Sheetrock and furniture and…well…people.

She'd wrapped both arms around his yellow Lab, Dorothy, so tight it was a wonder that Dorothy hadn't squirmed away or bitten her, but the dog seemed to know what she needed and had refused to leave her side.

Neither would Red. He'd hide her as long as he needed to.

He mentally ticked through all the stuff he was supposed to do tomorrow. Things he would have to put off. Ride his bike to the library. Catch a game of football with Doug Martin from two blocks over. Work on the book report for his English class on Monday. He was only halfway finished reading *Watership Down*.

I whispered to his little boy self. What did you say to me when you found me tonight? What did you say, exactly?

Nothing, the little boy whispered.

He'd grabbed me around the waist as I sneaked through his backyard, tucking a hand over my mouth as tight as he could without hurting me so that I wouldn't cry out.

What was my name? I asked.

Rosa, he said. The most beautiful name in the world.

Outside the closet, the world was on fire.

A sound so faint I shouldn't have been able to hear it from inside Red's memory raised my hackles. Animal instinct took over.

I let go of Red so fast, my magic rebounded like the business end of a slingshot—rocking me in my chair at the dinette. My vision blurred, my breath ragged. My hand twitched, knocking over my cup.

Instinct took over—I pivoted in my seat and ducked a half second later without knowing why.

It saved my life.

CHAPTER 2

THE BLADE ARCED over the top of my head, whisking through the strands of my hair and burying itself to the hilt in the Sheetrock.

For a moment, time slowed. Dust motes floated past my face. Shock threatened to numb me from the inside out as I stared at the one who'd thrown the knife. My daughter.

Faith met my gaze, her eyes filled with the kind of calculation that I'd only ever seen in another operative.

She'd never looked at me like that. She didn't know how.

Time sped up again. Everything happened too fast.

Red slipped from his seat, sliding beneath the table and out of the line of fire.

Sunday stood and flipped her chair in one fluid motion, launching it across the room at Faith with a precision she couldn't dodge. The full weight of the chair, with Sunday's muscle behind it, struck Faith in the center of the face as she dropped low behind the shield of the coffee table.

No way this could be my kid. No way had she learned to take body blow like that—or to move like that.

I mapped Faith's next moves as if she were a full-grown, full-fledged operative: Throw the table. Rush us. Avoid Sunday's line of sight at all costs. If Sunday could see her, Sunday could blind her.

Unlike Sunday, I didn't need a line of sight in order to take her. I needed only proximity and time. I reached for Faith's mind—and closed my mental fingers around nothing, as if I were trying to catch smoke with my bare hands. I sucked in a breath.

Faith's mind was slippery. Each entry point—a stray thought I could latch onto, a strategic ebb or flow, a focus on one or the other of us—slid out from under my magical grasp.

I flashed a glance at Sunday. She saw I didn't have control. She launched herself at Faith like a missile.

Faith picked up the table and charged.

Sunday hit the tabletop before Faith could get enough traction to push back. Faith backpedaled into the fireplace with a thud that shook the painting of Our Lady, frame rattling against the wall.

I grabbed for Faith's mind again, slip-sliding against her thoughts.

Sunday bounced back, dropped low, and swept Faith's legs.

Faith and the table went over like a felled tree. The table legs she'd white-knuckled snapped with the impact. Her forehead smacked into the underside of the teak.

I caught a single, stray memory at the edges of Faith's mind. One that she hadn't guarded as tightly as the others. One that I could wrap my magical fingers around.

She felt my reach. She fought against it, winding the memory this way and that, stealing it from my grasp. Once. Twice.

The third time was the charm.

I melded my magic with the rhythm of her winding. I slipped into the memory as if it were my own, struggling to gain purchase as if I were trying to grab hold of moss-covered rocks with my bare feet.

I became her.

I bobbed in a river, water raging all around me. The sky was dark, clouds dimming the light of the stars, a sign that God had left me in the cold and dark. I tried to swim. I couldn't make my arms work right. The spray off the surface blinded me. Rain fell in sheets. The wind gusted, wild and terrifying. My mouth filled with water. It tasted like death. I swallowed it and managed a mouthful of precious air before I sank below the rough surface.

I couldn't navigate the raging water. I couldn't push my way to the surface—which way was up? The icy cold of the river seeped through my skin, dragging my muscles, chilling me all the way to the depths of my bones.

It stole my will. It stole everything that made me who I was. All I needed was one breath of air. Just one. I pulled at the water with flailing arms. Nothing happened.

The water stung my eyes. I could barely see. Still, I forced my eyes to stay open. To keep myself among the living. If I gave up, I'd drown.

I understood all too well. I knew that river intimately. I'd seen it in my nightmares all week.

I knew how to twist the fear Faith felt. How to ratchet up the fear so high, it would stop her heart.

I grabbed hold of the river inside of her. Of the impossible, overwhelming pressure in her chest. Her body's instinct to breathe in, knowing that if she did, killing water would fill her lungs. She couldn't stop it. She couldn't save herself. She'd been brought there to the river to see whether she'd survive. She'd failed. She'd been brought there to die.

God wasn't coming to help her. No one would come. No one would save her.

She opened her mouth. Only a second—maybe two—before she drew in the killing breath.

I wrapped my magic around her like a vise. A grip that could not be broken. A deadly weight that could not be lifted. I squeezed.

Her thoughts rained on me, hard as bullets.

God isn't coming. No one coming. Not even the Rose.

The Rose of Death. That had been what my mentor in the Order called me—what everyone there had called me. Rose.

The operative masquerading as my daughter was remembering me. As if I'd been there the night she'd nearly died. In the river, being tested. An icy, rainy, windy hell, clouds soaring across the starry face of the night. The sadness inside her overwhelmed her fear of dying.

I stopped squeezing. I didn't let her go, but I didn't kill her.

Sunday's breath came fast and hard. "Is it Faith? It's not her. It can't be."

Nothing in the operative's memory reflected the slightest trace of my girl. The fact that they looked just like Faith, down to the finest detail, rocked me to the marrow.

I shook my head. "No, it's not my kid."

She glanced past the operative and me, toward Red. "You hurt?"

"No," he said. "What the hell's going on?"

"This is a chameleon," Sunday said. "Look, Red."

Red stepped toward us. "Holy Hell."

"It's more than that," I said. "I recognize him."

"Him?" Red asked.

At that moment, the body that looked like my daughter's began to shift. The face grew razor stubble and a square jaw. The chameleon grew taller—to around six-two. His arms thickened. His chest became wider, stronger. His black hair stretched several more inches, weaving itself together until it hung in a long braid to his waist. His halo had a peculiar purple cast to it, like a nasty bruise. Or a slick of oil, its sheen shifting and changing.

The clothes he'd worn—clothes that looked like Faith's—were so tight now, they cut off his circulation.

I moved toward Sunday and the chameleon, hunkering down beside them. I wanted to take the final step with the chameleon more than anything. Squeeze the life out of him. Leave him nothing but a sack of bones.

But there was something else going on here. Something that scared me almost as much.

How did chameleons copy other people's flesh and blood? How did they impersonate them so successfully? Did they have to touch their targets to do it? Did they have to kill them?

I spoke inside his mind. *Did you hurt Faith?*

The question hung suspended between us for a long moment. I held my breath.

No, he said.

It wasn't possible for him to lie to me while I had his mind in my grasp. At least, no one had ever been able to do so before.

Where is she? I asked.

With her friends, he said. *Safe and sound. I didn't touch a hair on her head.*

Inch by careful inch, I slipped from the depths of the chameleon's memory, keeping my hold on him secure as I began to split my attention between the chameleon's mind and my own. I didn't dare take my eyes off of him or loosen my grip, but I could sense Sunday well enough beside me—all of her now, not just her voice and breath.

Heat rose from her body, from the fight and from her magic, bridling beneath the surface and coiled to strike, her halo a spiral of crimson and gold. I felt Red in the far corner of the room, near the door to my bedroom. I could smell the grass and earth of his magic, the perfume of the wild world after a rain.

Sunday was talking. I honed in on her words.

"No surprise you recognize him," she said. "He's one of us. What's it matter?"

"I mean I *know* him," I said. "Or knew him. He's supposed to be dead."

Sunday fisted her hand around his braid and hauled his head up a couple of inches. He turned his face away from hers.

"Not going to blind you unless you ask for it," she said.

He mulled that over for a minute, then decided to take her at her word. He looked at her, deep brown eyes measuring carefully.

He had the cheekbones I remembered, and the same mouth. No smile lines—no frown lines, either. He'd rarely smiled when we'd known him. He'd saved those for when he felt safe.

When had we ever felt safe?

Sunday narrowed her eyes, studying the lines of his face. "Can't be."

Across the room, Red cleared his throat. "You want to tell me what's going on?"

The operative sighed. His voice was a sweet tenor, deeper than I remember, but then it would be. He was a man now.

"Hey," he said.

Impersonate my daughter, infiltrate my house, try to kill me—and all he had to offer was *Hey?* Jesus.

"Miguel," I said.

"Miguel?" Red asked. "Miguel from the nightmare this morning?"

"Yes," I said.

I'd mourned him all those years ago, after the mentors had picked up Sunday and me from the dock at the riverside, soaked and shivering and half-drowned.

The ride back to the base in the van with no windows had been somber. Sunday, wrapped in a dark green Army surplus blanket, had drawn her knees to her chest and put her head down. She'd been a world unto herself. I'd stared, stone-faced, at the floor of the van, fixated on a slew of pebbles that rolled on the matted dark gray carpet with every bump and turn. I'd shrugged off the blanket the mentors had given me. If I'd been cold, I hadn't felt it at all. I hadn't felt anything except the vibration from the engine and the roll of the tires on pavement.

After we returned, the mentors put each of us in separate, sterile rooms with walls so white, they practically glowed in the dark. The full-sized bed swallowed me. The weight of the white cotton sheets and the single white wool blanket were too stifling. I couldn't stand the feel of them. It took some time before the cold that remained inside of me surfaced on my skin and the fine hairs on my arms rose like antennae, and some time after that before I pulled up the covers. It took even longer for the first tear to well in my eye.

I had so few people I liked. So few people I could count on. Now I had one less. And whatever Miguel had hoped would happen to him— whatever dreams he'd had—they'd slipped to the bottom of the river along with him.

Sunday sneaked out of her room and into mine, heaven only knew how—rules didn't apply to her. She'd crawled into bed with me and wrapped me in her arms while I shook, the heat of her magic rising from her body then the way it did now. She'd held me until sleep overtook me. She was still holding me when I woke.

I blinked away the memory. I looked hard at the man on my floor, superimposing the face and body of the Miguel I'd known. He'd had super-strength back then, with a halo like steel. He was still damn strong, but his strength didn't seem as daunting to me as it had before, and now his halo shone purple, a shimmer blurring its edges.

I didn't understand.

People's halos didn't change. People were born with a certain quality of life force—particular talents, skills, and abilities that reflected the core of who they were—and no matter what else changed about them, the character of their life force, of their halos, never did.

"You sure he's not faking?" Sunday asked. "This isn't some kind of chameleon trick?"

I shook my head.

"His memories?" she asked.

I wasn't infallible. It was possible I was wrong, but I didn't think so. I'd stake my life on it—that was what we were talking about here, to be clear. My life, and everyone else's. "They're real."

I met Miguel's gaze. "Where's the Order been hiding you all these years?"

He hesitated.

Sunday pulled his head back a little more. He winced. She grinned.

"You know hurting me won't get you anywhere," he said.

"I know," she said. "I'm just enjoying myself."

Miguel's mouth curved in a half-smile. His eyes lit with it exactly the way I remembered. "You haven't changed at all."

"You have," I said. "The life force you carry has been altered."

His smile faded. "Caught that, did you?"

"Your super-strength," I said. "Where's it gone?"

"Away," he said. "They took most of it and used it to make me into something else."

I didn't think that could be done either, but I was staring at the evidence.

"Why am I still alive?" he asked.

"Because of who you used to be," I said.

"Because of who I used to be to you, you mean."

I held his gaze.

"Kill me and get it over with," he said.

I looked at Sunday. Her eyes and the set of her mouth hardened. She pulled Miguel's head back a little further, then slammed it down again into the remains of the table.

He blacked out.

Red took a cautious step toward us. "What now?"

"Now we take him to my place and tie him up," Sunday said. "See what we can get out of him."

"We should get him outta here now," Red said. "That was a lot of ruckus for early on a Sunday morning. Chances are, y'all woke at least one of the neighbors."

The good news was that someone would knock before they'd call the cops. The bad news was that someone would knock.

Not a second later, my phone chimed from its spot on the night-stand. Incoming text. I could guess who'd sent it—the only one of the neighbors with my number. She'd exchanged contact info with me the day after Faith and I had moved in, saying we women needed to watch out for each other. She'd keep an eye on my place if I kept an eye on hers.

Red ran to grab the phone without being asked. He replied to the text on his way back into the front room. "Telling her a friend's visit-ing. Fell and broke the coffee table. Seems fine, but we'll be leaving in a minute to get them checked out anyway. Sorry for the noise, blah blah."

"Nice work," I said.

"You want to carry Miguel out the door, you got cover," Red said.

I stuck out my hand. "Phone."

He passed it to me. I put the phone on speaker and dialed at light speed.

Faith picked up just before the call went to voice mail. She sounded groggy, as if I'd woken her. "Night? What's up?"

I exhaled a shuddering breath, pressing a hand to my heart. "Where are you?"

"The usual," she said. "Ben's."

Ben's house was hangout central. They could talk about magic there. Practice all they wanted. Get themselves into trouble. All without the prying eyes of parents, given that Ben's dad traveled all the time. Ben's place was also a couple of blocks from Red's gym, where Red had planned to head after breakfast. One class on the schedule today.

I didn't want Faith to come home. The Order would send a follow-up crew, and the apartment would be the first stop. That made the gym the closest safe space.

Red closed the distance between us. "Stay there. I'll pick you up on the way to the gym."

The sleep vanished from her voice. "What's wrong?"

"The Order," I said.

Her voice shook. "You're okay?"

"We're fine. We're taking care of it. The operative they sent is a chameleon, Faith."

I'd told her about chameleons, just like every other type of operative we could run into. Forewarned, forearmed.

"Is?" she asked.

Sunday set her hands on her hips. "He's not dead yet, kiddo. Have a little faith."

Faith usually laughed at that, but not this time. "I'll tell the others."

I hoped the other kids were ready. I hoped Faith was. "Just be careful, all right?"

"I love you, too, Night." Faith hung up.

"Thank God," Red said.

"I'll do my thanking when I lay eyes on her," I said.

Sunday stood up and fished her keys out of her front pocket. "Red, can you go get my car and bring it up to the back lot? It's two blocks west on the left side of the street. White Mustang."

He looked from her to me and back again. It was plain on his face that he felt we weren't telling him something. He was right.

"It's okay," I said.

He raised a brow that told me he expected to hear whatever it was later, come hell or high water. Only after I nodded did he shove his feet into the pair of dark blue sneakers he kept by the front door and shrug on his coat.

Sunday waited a long minute after the door closed behind him before she rubbed her forehead with the heels of her hands, smoothing her blond curls away from her face. "If Miguel had really wanted to hit you, he'd have waited until I left, or until you were alone. Anyone else here, even if it's Red, and his odds get worse. So why bother with this half-assed shit? Calling me in? Not to mention bringing one knife. What gives?"

The last time the Order had sent an operative after us, we'd discovered one very important change that had been made since we'd been gone. The Order had begun magically programming its operatives to obey instead of threatening them into it. That had to have been done to Miguel. He'd have to make an attempt to fulfill his mission. He'd have no choice.

But he'd also have known who the Order sent him to take out. We'd been friends, real friends, a lifetime ago. How did he feel about that? Did he feel anything? If it was me, I would have. So maybe he'd made this half-assed try, to use Sunday's word, and he'd failed. The Order would have to know by now.

I sucked in a breath. The Order was in Miguel's mind. I'd been in his mind. It had been second nature, survival instinct. They'd have expected that, used it.

"Sunday, we've got a problem."

"Just one?" she asked.

"Maybe the mission wasn't to kill us after all. Maybe the mission was to get a peek inside my head."

She stared at me. "Shit, Night."

"It wouldn't take much time to get a read on me. To get a glimpse into my thoughts, my strategy, my hopes and fears."

"If they didn't know about the Angel of Death trapped in your head before, they'd know about it now."

I pushed up from a crouch and perched on the edge of the sofa, resting my elbows on my knees. I felt a little sick, going from an easy morning in bed with my lover to a battle in my own living room with a man I'd believed to be dead. And now, this.

"We're going to have company sooner or later," she said.

"I'd hoped for later."

Sunday shrugged. It was all the same to her. Then she cocked her head. "You told him his life force had been altered."

I nodded. "He has the purple halo and the shimmer around the edges. And he's still stupid strong, but not as strong as I'd expect someone like him to be by now."

"The Order kept him hidden from us all these years. They wanted the rest of us to think he was dead. What were they doing with him—to him—during that time?" she asked.

Exactly. To take someone off the grid by removing them from the world, training them to become an operative who lived a secret life, in the shadows, was a thing. To remake an Order operative completely? That was some next-level shit.

"How does someone become a chameleon?" I asked.

"All this time, I've been thinking they were born that way, like I said before," Sunday said. "What if my information is wrong, though? What if they're not born? What if they're created?"

I looked at Miguel, so peaceful in his unconsciousness. If a person's magic could be altered from its original design, if it could be spliced or transformed into something else, what would that do to a person? How long would it take?

Not days or weeks. Not even months. If it could be done at all, that kind of thing would take years. A lot of years.

"Damn," I said.

"Normally, I'd be all about your doing what you need to do and catching up with me later, but maybe in this case you and Red should close the gym for the day."

I checked the time on my phone. "Not everyone will get the message in time. People will show up."

She shrugged.

"If the Order is watching the gym—"

"The Order won't care about a bunch of gym rats," she said.

She was right. "They were after me, and there's no point in advertising their presence in front of a bunch of normals just to get my attention."

The door opened as she sighed. "My point exactly."

I glanced behind her to see Red on his way back in. "Everything okay out there?"

"Yeah," Red said. "You're going with Sunday and the chameleon, aren't you?"

I nodded. "Let me get ready. I'll be out in a sec."

I headed for the bedroom. As soon as I crossed the threshold, out of sight of the others, a tremor started in my legs. It was slight—nothing bothersome or obvious—just adrenaline processing through now that the immediate threat had passed. The light that had warmed the bed as Red and I woke had faded. The room felt cold and empty, the rumpled sheets and comforter a reminder that the peace of the morning had been shattered, and might not return.

Eventually, my inner voice said. Eventually it would.

But the rest of me didn't quite believe it. I'd lived under the watchful eye of death or on the run for so long, there wasn't anything else, not really. At that thought, something brushed the inside of my chest, just to the left of my heart.

Heartburn from the coffee, or from the attempt on our lives?

It didn't feel like heartburn. It felt like something that didn't belong to me, but that lived inside me. The exact sensation was difficult to put into words. My inner voice supplied a description that sent a shiver up my spine from my tailbone to the crown of my head: the brush of the Angel's wings against the inside of my rib cage.

Which had to be bullshit. The Angel was where I'd put him last month, locked tight in a cage inside my mind. Any fluttering in my chest was flesh-and-blood fluttering, and nothing more.

Unless it wasn't.

I couldn't ignore the feeling, or the fear it woke in me. I'd have to do something about it. What, I didn't know. For now, I shook off the feeling as best I could and marched for the dresser, pulling out clean panties and a bra, followed by black chinos and a long-sleeved black T-shirt. Clothes that could hide blood if they needed to.

I looked up as I heard Red step into the room. His expression was careful. The lines at the corners of his eyes seemed deeper than they'd been just an hour ago.

He snicked the door shut behind him. "Tell me," he said.

Not yet. "First you show me."

He let me into his mind again without a word of protest. I searched for a chameleon in him, but found none. He was himself. Just Red.

Relief washed through me, then washed away. I turned my back to the dresser, shoving the drawer closed with my hip. "I'm in trouble, Red. Sunday and I think the Order were using Miguel as bait."

He pieced it together fine. "Not to kill you," he said. "But so you'd use your magic on him."

I nodded.

"What do you need?" he asked.

For time to run in reverse. To be in bed with him, drowsy and coming to after a good night's sleep. To wake to him again, with time enough to make love. To have had more hours and days and weeks before the Order came calling.

"Take care of Faith. Make sure she's safe. Don't get hurt."

"I'll do my best." He closed the space between us. Just a handful of steps. Each one felt momentous to me, as if he was about to say or do something that would change everything.

"I checked Sunday just now, just like she asked before. I'll check Faith when I see her. Make sure everyone is who they claim to be." He paused. When he spoke again, I could hear his magic in his voice. "You're not, though."

Whatever I'd expected to hear, that wasn't it. "I'm not a chameleon."

He shook his head. "No, you're not. But you're not the same Night you were before the Angel came to town. I see him inside of you."

I held his gaze. "You haven't told me that before. Why?"

"Wasn't true before. I knew he was in here"—he tapped a finger on my temple—"but I didn't *see* him. Now, I do."

"Since when?" I asked.

"Since this morning. He's stirring," Red said. "It scares me."

I fought the impulse to press a hand to my chest where I'd felt the feather-brush only moments ago. "Me, too."

He framed my face with his hands. "Be careful, Night."

I leaned into him, lifting his hands from my face, lowering them into place around my waist. I rose up on my toes and kissed him, tasting his natural sweetness and the richness of coffee and cream. His hands traveled along the curve of my back to tangle in my hair. He drew me closer. I breathed him in, as if by taking in the scent and taste of him, I could take a part of him with me.

Even pulling away, he kept his eyes locked on mine. "You call me as soon as you know something."

"I promise," I said.

He took a step back, freeing me to peel off my tank and jeans and dress for the mission at hand. He watched me boldly, gaze moving along the contours of my skin the whole time. As I pulled on the last item—the T-shirt—I heard his voice, muffled by the fabric.

"Is that what former assassins are wearing on the job these days?"

I laughed. I couldn't help it. Tension had wound my so tight inside, I needed a little release. "It's what all the magic-users are wearing these days. Allows the fashionable magician to move seamlessly between war with the Order and dinner out with your sweetie." I tugged the hem of the shirt into place, then combed my hair with my fingers.

"Don't let Miguel get to you," he said.

I sat on the bed, pulling on thick wool socks and shoving my feet into black, steel-toed boots, completing my assassin fashion. "I think it's a little late for that, don't you?"

"Not what I meant. He's not who he used to be, Night."

That was the obvious thing to say. But whatever Red was, he wasn't about the obvious. He hadn't been in the room for Sunday's and my chameleon conversation. All I could think was that if the

Order had altered Miguel's magic, they might have altered his personality. Or he might have had experiences that had changed him utterly. All of that was true. But Red was talking about emotion. About feeling I might once have had for Miguel. It was what had stayed my hand out there.

"He might not deserve that much consideration," Red said.

I needed to remember that. "Understood."

Red held my gaze a moment, then nodded.

"I have a practical request," I said. "Got any spare clothes you want to donate to the cause?"

"For Miguel?" he asked.

"He's conspicuous as hell, wearing Faith's outfit."

"I find myself wanting to know how he got a hold of her clothes," Red said.

One hundred percent. "You're not the only one."

I waited for him to put something together, then led the way into the living room with Red on my heels. Sunday was bent over Miguel, a syringe in her hand.

I cracked a small smile. Miguel-as-Faith had called Sunday with an emergency, after all. What did a former Order operative bring to an emergency?

"Hide that in your coat?" I asked.

Sunday nodded.

"Your gun, too?" I asked.

"Like I had time to go for that," she said.

Just like old times.

Sunday shrugged. "Be prepared."

Red shook his head. "The things they don't teach you in the Scouts. How long will he stay out?"

Sunday plunged the needle into Miguel's neck. "Couple of hours, give or take. Plenty of time to transport and get him set up."

Plenty of time? No such thing. "And dress him."

Now that the threat of immediate violence had passed and we had a plan, I couldn't help but think about what could've happened if I'd been a split-second later with my reaction time—what Miguel might've done to the people I loved, what could still happen to them if we weren't careful.

I couldn't help wondering whether, even with the formidable skill set Sunday and I had between the two of us, we were in over our heads with Miguel.

My head discounted that thought completely. We had everything under control.

My heart didn't believe that for a minute.

CHAPTER 3

S UNDAY'S BASEMENT LOOKED and felt like a souvenir from
our time in the Order. It had been unfinished when she moved
in two weeks ago, nothing but a concrete floor and concrete walls
stinking of mothballs, lit by long, thin fluorescents that washed the
color out of everything and everyone. The washer and dryer, water
heater, and furnace had looked forlorn, like lonely children banished
to the corner for bad behavior.

In the time since she'd moved, she hadn't done much with the
parts of the house most people considered important. Instead, she'd
spent time getting ready for trouble on the way. She'd been goddamn
busy.

She'd installed some company for the sullen appliances in the form
of three metal kennels large enough to hold a Great Dane—or a
handful of Order operatives. She'd hung thick black foam baffling on
the walls and the ceiling. She'd outfitted the space with three metal
chairs, one of which she'd bolted to the floor in the middle of the
room. She'd pulled all the light fixtures except one, situated just overhead. She'd brought down a metal kitchen cart outfitted with a few
essential pieces—white plastic zip ties, a scalpel, a saw, a pair of pliers,
a jug of water, a stack of thick white terrycloth towels.

She didn't need any of the weapons, of course. She was a weapon. But who knew when the threat she'd use them might come in handy? Definitely a scream-all-you-want situation for anyone unlucky enough to become her prisoner.

All of that aside, there was one more essential thing Sunday had done to outfit her basement to handle whatever the Order, or anyone else, sent our way: layers of magical protection. A film of invisibility set into the walls, floor, and ceiling that I could see the same way I could see people's halos. It shimmered like a heat wave over a road in high summer. Above that, a set of wards had been locked into place, as hard and cold as a set of steel doors The layer on top of that, closest to the interior of the room, acted as a mirror. It reflected back all magic sent toward it.

This place was hard, if not impossible, for another magician to see. Even if they could, they'd have to breach the shield of energetic steel. For anyone inside the space, good luck sending out a message or a signal.

Sunday had made the basement as safe as she could, the equivalent of a magical Faraday cage. Good thing, too. We needed it now.

Together, Sunday and I poured Miguel's limp body into the bolted chair, stripping off his black-and-gray plaid shirt, but leaving him with the modesty and warmth of his black turtleneck for the time being. He was heavier than he looked. Moving him left me winded.

Sunday wasn't breathing hard, but her skin was flushed pink with the effort. She slipped out of her black trench, letting it fall to the floor. Wisps of blond curls stuck to her cheeks. She brushed them away, tucking them behind her ears. Plucking a rubber band from her pocket, she reached up to tuck her unruly hair into a loose bun that perched precariously on the top of her head.

All told, it had taken us half an hour to get Miguel loaded into the car and over to Sunday's. No one had looked askance at us on the drive. If Sunday's neighbors had noticed us helping our unconscious friend up the sidewalk beneath the dripping needles of the fir trees in her yard, they'd kept it to themselves.

It was almost as if we were charmed.

The feeling hit me hard enough to give me pause. It wasn't something I would normally think or feel.

I believed in intuition. I believed in trusting my gut. Those things were tools, just like my magic, or Sunday's gun, which she'd migrated from her coat to her waistband—she had no desire to encounter another need and not have it on her for backup.

"This is too good to be true," I said.

She waved off my concern.

"In broad daylight. In a city. With the Order tracking us," I said.

She met my gaze. "We're as good as we'll ever be right here."

True. But. "Something's off."

"Maybe so. What say we wake this asshole up and find out?"

I sighed. "Safety first. Pass me some zip ties."

She tossed me one and took the other herself. We cuffed Miguel's hands to the chair legs. I pulled mine tight enough to cut off his circulation.

He looked so peaceful in his stillness. Not deadly at all. A thin coat of mud streaked the toes of his black boots, as if he'd simply been careless while walking instead of having been dragged across rain-soaked earth. His head lolled to the left, his breathing slow and steady. His long, braided black hair had absorbed its share of rain, enough to create a slow trickle of water down the back of his shirt. He had a serious set of bags under his eyes—hadn't slept well, if at all, for a few days.

Miguel's halo still had the strange, bruised purple cast. It no longer shifted or changed as I watched, maybe because he was unconscious. I didn't know enough about chameleons to understand the whys and wherefores of their life force and how it looked.

I pulled off my coat, draping it over the back of the closest empty chair, while Sunday pulled the jug of water from the kitchen cart, uncapped it, and splashed him across the face. He sputtered awake, a shiver running in a wave from the crown of his head to the soles of his feet.

"Afternoon," Sunday said.

He peered at her, his dark brown pupils dilated, seeming to crowd out the whites of his eyes.

"So, you're all grown up," she said.

He cleared his throat. His words were tinged with disdain. "You ever get what you wanted from Night? Make her yours?"

"You never liked me," she said. "The feeling's mutual, so I'm gonna let your tone slide."

He tried on a half-smile, but couldn't quite make it work. "I was your competition."

"Damn right," Sunday said.

Oh, for fuck's sake.

I'd loved them both from the get-go. I'd never cared whether they liked each other. I'd only been glad to have both of them in those first days of confusion after the Order had brought us into the fold, and in the time that came after. When you're being trained to kill, and people you came to care about occasionally disappeared without a trace or died because they couldn't make the cut, the whole world became death. Having a little light to hold onto was a lifeline.

"Well," I said. "Now that we've established our feelings, I have some questions." I hunkered down in front of Miguel so that he didn't have to look up to see my face. To see me. If he had any feelings for me after all these years—and he certainly was playing that angle—I might be able to take advantage of them.

He held my gaze. "Ask me all about the Order's plans. You know I won't be able to tell you anything critical."

Not at the top of my list. "How did you get close enough to Faith to copy her?"

"Easiest thing in the world to find her and her friends at the coffee shop," he said. "I took a seat at the next table."

Normal teenager thing, picking up a coffee drink with more sugar than the human body can handle and hanging out with her friends. She would've given the place the once-over, checking for anyone who looked suspicious—that was still second nature. We hadn't been in Portland long enough for her to have lost her *on the run* habits.

Miguel wouldn't have looked suspicious in the least. It was his nature to blend in.

"And her clothes?" I asked.

"I took them from her friend's place. The redhead with the white cat."

"If I find out you hurt her, you're dead," I said.

"She's not your daughter," he said. "Not really. How can you care so much?"

I stared at him. "How long has it been since you cared about anyone? Since anyone cared about you?"

He averted his gaze.

"What happened to you?" I asked. "We thought you died that night. That you drowned."

He shook his head, then winced. The sedative Sunday had given him packed a punch. "I never went into the water," he said. "The mentors pushed you in, then grabbed me and tossed me into a waiting van. I thought I was being culled."

Those occasional disappearances happened when a trainee didn't measure up, when the Order had no use for them, not even as diversions or as proverbial cannon fodder. But what had happened to Miguel didn't fit the MO for culling. He'd been about to be pushed into the river along with Sunday and me. He hadn't been disappeared. The mentors had wanted us to think he was dead.

"Where did they take you?" I asked.

He studied the floor for a moment before looking back at me. "Back to HQ."

Where the rest of us lived and trained. "How's that possible? We never saw you again."

"You think you know everything about that place?" he asked.

"I know I don't," I said. There were places only mentors had clearance to enter, for instance. I had ideas about how much space their inner sanctum comprised, but clearly my ideas were bullshit.

"There are whole areas that function separate and apart from the main facility." He lowered his voice so that I had to listen carefully to hear. "Places that aren't entirely in this world."

Sunday bent, resting her hands on her thighs. "What does that mean, exactly?"

"It means exactly what I said. Those places are interfaces between the human world and other worlds. Realms where the crazy shit lives. Demons. Faeries."

We'd been taught about the other beings. About the kinds of magical law enforcement that kept them in line when they entered the human world. The mild surprise on Sunday's face masked a deeper shock that I could read in her because I knew her so well.

I felt it, too. The idea that the Order's headquarters was only partially located in the human world was news—the kind of news that fell into place like the missing piece of a puzzle.

The Angel of Death was the secret head of the Order. If he'd had a place within the confines of the Order's headquarters, it wouldn't have been in the human world.

I narrowed my eyes at Miguel. "Did you live in one of those spaces —in another realm? And they made you into a chameleon there?"

"They make all chameleons," he said. "We can only be created in a place like that, in the In-Between. It's an inhuman place, or at least a place where humans shouldn't go. Dangerous. Full of desperate things —like a bunch of teenage assassin wannabes being tortured and shaped into new magical creatures."

"Is that how you see yourself?" I asked.

He didn't answer that question right away. "The two mentors who watched you and Sunday that night, the night of the water, he stayed with you, right? But a third one, that guy took me back to HQ and down a set of concrete stairs that eventually turned to hand-carved stone. They were steep and too tall for human legs. I fell twice. Got all scraped up. Bloody knuckles. Bloody knees. I was scared out of my mind."

I had the urge to cut through the words and slip into his mind so I could see the place he was talking about and feel what he felt. So I wouldn't just hear what he said, and assume. So I would know.

The impulse hit me so strongly, I'd begun to open my magic and reach for his mind before I realized I'd done it. Even though I figured that in entering his mind before, I'd given the Order precious access to my mind. Even though I shouldn't take the chance again.

He was *sending* to me, feeding me emotions and triggering impulses.

I pulled the power back into myself, making sure it was anchored and wouldn't stray again. I flexed my fingers, then curled my hands into fists.

"You really want to play it like that?" I asked.

"Sorry," he said, in a tone that told me he felt anything but. "It's my mission. Anyhow, the stone staircase for giants led to this black wall of energy. Not black like it had substance, but black like it was nothing—literally nothing. Passing through it was like waking through fire. It was burning hot and there was no air. It only took a minute to cross, but that minute felt like forever. It felt like Hell, or like I thought Hell would feel. Then we were in the In-Between, and all I could smell was sulfur. The stink was so thick, it coated everything. That place, it looks like our world. But it feels like a shadow."

Part of me bought it. The rest of me wondered how much deeper he was trying to draw me in.

"How're you able to say all of this?" The Order would have programmed his mind. Magical chains.

"Did you sense chains in my mind when you were in there?" he asked.

"I wasn't looking for them." But if Miguel's mental conditioning followed what I'd seen before, they'd have been there, and they wouldn't have been all that hard to spot.

"Chameleons don't have them," he said. "Angel's orders. No one can survive the In-Between without full mental and physical function."

I glanced at Sunday. She met my gaze, my thoughts mirrored behind her eyes. How had all of this gone on inside the Order without more people knowing about it?

"You lived there all this time?" I asked.

"There and one other place," he said.

I raised a brow.

He shrugged as best he could, tied up like he was. "I'm surprised you haven't figured it out already with what you got inside you."

I glared at him.

"Don't treat me like I'm stupid," he said.

I felt a momentarily flutter of a thousand wings inside my gut. It had to be the Angel.

I'd known from the get-go that the Order would realize eventually what had happened to the Angel. Who in the human realm had enough power to make a being like that vanish without a trace?

I hadn't thought it would be me. But there it was.

Then again, Miguel had said *I*, not *we*. Miguel, not the Order.

"Just you?" I asked.

"The chameleons. We know what's up."

"All that time you spent in the Angelic realm?" I asked.

His mouth curved into a half-grin. "Someone had to be closest to the Angel. Be the ones who took his orders and filtered them down to the leadership, through the mentors, to the rest of you."

Sunday whistled softly. "You expect us to believe that?"

I glanced at her. From the look on her face, she did believe it in her heart. The rest of her needed convincing.

"You of all people know what it's like to be close to him, Night," Miguel said.

Sunday sighed, rising to her full height. "I'm about at my bullshit threshold already."

"Everything he's told us could be the truth. Or could not," I said.

"I'll be all about finding out for sure," she said.

She could make him afraid. She could make him wish he were dead. She couldn't make him tell her anything. Besides, he'd already told us a ton.

"What are you really doing?" I asked. "If you'd wanted us dead bad enough, one of us would be cold by now. If you'd wanted to spin a story to pull me in, you wouldn't have tipped your hand the way you did."

He didn't answer—not out loud. Thoughts spun behind his eyes, though.

Sunday nudged me with an elbow. "Why don't you update Red?"

I glanced at her. She wore her best making-a-suggestion-that-was-more-like-an-order expression. Eyebrows raised. Mouth firm. Jaw set.

It'd been a while since I'd tortured someone. I still remembered how, and I'd have no problem. I protected the people I loved, whatever it took. I told her as much with one look.

She shook her head once. Her lips curved in a slight smile. It took me a second to understand what she was really trying to say. She didn't doubt me at all. She knew I could get the job done as well as she could—maybe too well, given my rising temper. But she didn't want me to.

When I'd left the life behind, I'd meant it. Any harm I'd done since, I'd done to protect Faith. Sunday had left the Order to protect me, but she'd never renounced the violence.

I'd chosen to change in fundamental ways that she hadn't. Better that I didn't go back down that road. Better not to prove Miguel right. Not unless I had no choice.

I looked at him long and hard, gazing into his dark brown eyes. "Why don't you check his story? I've heard all I want to hear for now."

I spun on my heel, grabbed my coat, and headed for the stairs. The muffled fall of my steps kept time with my heartbeat.

I didn't have to keep eyes on Miguel to know how he prepared for whatever torture Sunday could cook up. I'd been in his exact position, in some dank basement with homemade soundproofing—or something like it—my wrists and ankles cuffed to a chair that had seen plenty of others like me. He'd make it through most, if not all, of what Sunday dished out. Whatever he chose to say, he'd get the payback for attempted murder that he deserved.

This wasn't about me. I didn't want to die just yet, but I'd planned for the contingency, and in my line of work—hell, my whole life—I'd expected it to happen suddenly and without grace.

Miguel had come into my home in the presence of my man, who was innocent in all of this but nevertheless was grown and held power in his own right. Red made his own decisions, and if he'd tied his fate to mine, that was his business. If he had to pay a price for that, he'd come to terms with it already. And Sunday was, well, Sunday.

But my daughter? I didn't care that she carried a latent god inside of her. Faith was a kid. She was my kid.

Miguel's voice rang out behind me. "Night."

I paused my step.

"You know you have to be something more than human to survive the Angel's magic being used against you, much less to contain it the way you're doing."

I knew no such thing. I didn't want to hear another word about being something less—or more—than human. I'd spent all of my extremely short childhood hearing some version of it.

"What are you, *hermana?*" he asked.

I didn't so much as glance over my shoulder. "You wanted to be my brother, you wouldn't have drawn steel in the presence of my family. You wouldn't have copied my daughter—and she *is* my kid. Make no mistake."

He took that in and mulled it over. I could tell from the quality of his silence. "You're right. But it wasn't an accident, how I came at you."

I continued to head for the staircase, a thread of panic weaving with the anger I felt.

No accident.

He could've taken his shot when I was alone in the apartment, put me down, and gone on his way without ever having to encounter anyone connected to me. Instead, he'd put himself in front of Sunday. In front of Red. He'd tried for me, but he'd wanted us all.

Miguel raised his voice with each word. "Back in the day, you'd have done the same thing."

Damn right, I would've. It was my job, my life. I had a different life now.

"How can you stand it?" he asked.

I glanced over my shoulder. His face held a mixture of pain and need. The emotions looked and felt real.

Miguel meant how could I stand having a daughter. A family. How could I let myself be vulnerable to the kind of loss that could break my heart—maybe kill me.

He wanted what I had, and it terrified him.

He'd meant to kill not just me, but my people.

I pulled my phone from my pocket and checked for a signal. Nothing down here, not with Sunday's protections in place. I took the stairs two at a time, shoving open the basement door and pushing it closed behind me with the heel of my boot. The close quarters of the hall I stepped into felt claustrophobic. Narrow space. Close, white walls. Dimmed light. The hardwood floor creaked underfoot. I had a signal on my phone instantly.

I jogged through the empty living room, racing out the front door into the icy afternoon rain, digging the car keys from my pocket. My blue Honda waited where I'd left it, parked at the curb behind Sunday's Mustang.

Red picked up on the fourth ring, hard rock blaring from the sound system in the background. His normally gentle drawl had grown deep with concern. "Night? What's going—"

I interrupted. "You and Faith okay?"

"Yes," he said.

"Anyone else there right now?"

He lowered his voice. "The last class ended a few minutes ago. We got one straggler, packing up slow. New guy."

New guy. Today of all days.

"What's the new guy look like?" I asked.

"He's just shy of six feet, strong as an ox, and drenched in sweat."

Like half the people who came in for classes. He could be just anybody, but I didn't like our odds. Not with him hanging back.

"Get out now," I said. "Both of you. I'm on my way."

"Is it another chameleon?" he asked.

"Now, Red."

I heard another voice on the other end of the phone. Not a man's voice, but Faith's.

I heard a loud thud and a clatter—Red's phone hitting the floor. A muffled grunt followed, and then a scream.

Faith's scream.

CHAPTER 4

I SKIDDED TO A STOP in front of the gym. Nothing looked out of place out here. No sign of a fight.

The neighborhood had the usual Sunday late-afternoon feel. Not too much traffic speeding by on Burnside. People out walking, bundled in coats with hoods raised against the drizzle. Across the way, the Stumptown Diner did laid back but respectable business, perfuming the air with the rich aromas of dark-roasted coffee, salty, crisp bacon, and fresh-baked bread. The maples in front of the diner had been wrapped in white Christmas lights that glowed with warmth.

I reached out with my magic, scanning for anyone lying in wait. Nothing.

The gym's big window remained intact. No breaks in or smears on the glass. The door was closed. Unusual in decent weather during the winter, but not alarming. The sidewalk held no traps. But the space in front of the door was black. Scorched.

I pushed my way into the narrow front room of the gym. The electronic bell above the door chimed. I took a deep breath of rubber, bleach wipes, and sweat. The normal smells. Underneath it all, the reek of sulfur.

Miguel had said the In-Between stank of sulfur.

I felt the urge to call out, intense and demanding. I needed to run in.

I forced myself not to. To let my training kick in.

If I ran into an ambush because of fear, I wouldn't be able to help anyone. One step at a time. Clear the gym in sections. I let my magic flow in front of me like an incoming tide, water rolling over everything in its path, tendrils of foam reaching further to touch what lay even further ahead.

I locked the front door behind me.

One of the overhead fluorescents dimmed for a second, buzzing, before it brightened again. No traps in here. The interlocked black rubber mats that covered the concrete floor appeared undisturbed. The triple-stacked row of black plastic cubbies and lockers that covered the long wall in front of me were empty. The old brown suede sofa crouched on the right.

The fine hairs on my arms stood straight up. The floor felt more solid beneath my feet, and my legs heavier, as if I had magnets on the bottoms of my boots. My breath came shallow.

Residual magic. Impressions of the last magician who'd walked in the space. Not a regular at the gym, or I'd have recognized them. Not an Order operative I'd known from my time there either. No one I knew.

I crossed the floor silently, taking the short staircase onto the gym floor.

The place was the size of a decent-sized basketball court, and it too was empty except for the equipment that hugged the scuffed, once-upon-a-white walls. Barbells pegged into metal stands, kettle bells, weight racks, and benches. Pull-up bars, medicine balls, wooden boxes for jumping. Some of it providing places for an assailant to hide.

I didn't sense anyone, but the back of my neck prickled.

I came to Red's office, on the left. No one sat in the chair behind the desk. The laptop was open, screen dark. One guest chair held Faith's black backpack. She'd hung her coat on the chair back.

Two steps beyond the office, I froze. The mat in front of me was wet. Hard to tell with what. Black masked every other color. Could be sweat. Could be someone spilled their water bottle. But I knew in my gut that was wishful thinking.

I hunkered down just long enough to drag a finger across the mat. It came away smeared with red.

Whose blood? Faith's? Red's? If one of them—

I shut down the thought before it could fully form.

I swallowed hard and got moving again toward the back, closer to the rowing machines that stood on end, like soldiers at attention. The two climbing ropes that hung from the ceiling swayed. A second later, the breeze that had moved them played across my face.

The garage doors that made up the entire back wall had been raised an inch. Gray light flooded in through the opening. Shadows moved on the other side of the doors.

I moved fast then, avoiding the play of light on the mats, staying on my toes and sticking close to the wall. I headed for the door furthest from the shadows, passing two empty bathrooms. The closer I drew to the door, the clearer I could make out what I saw on the other side: Red's dark blue sneaks and Faith's black hikers.

He stood in front of her, putting her back to the red brick wall of the building, shielding her from whoever might come at them from any direction—the gym, the back parking lot, or the street beyond. I sent my magic forward, looking for any danger I could find. Nothing. No one.

I bent down and got my fingers under the door. I yanked upwards, raising the door on its tracks. It thundered up all the way, slamming stop with a bang.

Red flinched. His green and earth halo seemed burnt around the edges. Blood streaked his right cheek and the fringe of his salt-and-pepper hair. Most of the right sleeve had been ripped from his white T-shirt. What remained hung by a thread. The left knee of his gym pants was torn.

He stood dead center on the three feet of jutting concrete that had once been the end of a loading dock. His eyes darted to the edge, and the four feet he'd fall if he went over.

I couldn't see Faith behind him, only the edges of her halo. The clean, clear silver of it told me the most important thing I needed to know. They were banged up, but they were all right.

I scanned the back lot. No cars and no people, just a bunch of tall weeds cozied up to the chain-link fence that ran down either side, waving in the wind. A single vehicle drove by on the street—an orange Subaru filled with teenage girls. The radio blared a song I'd heard Faith play before.

We were alone, the three of us.

Thank God.

Red held up a hand. "She's not hurt."

I met his gaze. He looked like himself. Like the man I knew and loved. I had to be sure. I slid my magic into his mind and probed there, rifling through thoughts and memories to make sure my senses didn't deceive.

He went still. He didn't move so much as a muscle. He didn't try to fight me, either. He let me do what needed to be done.

When I let him go, he sucked in a breath.

"You check her?" I asked.

He nodded.

I tried to peer around him to get a look at Faith. He saw that I craned my neck, but he didn't move out of the way. He took another step back, closer to her. Shielding her from me.

"You want to look at me? Make sure I am who I look like?" I asked. "Go ahead."

We couldn't take any chances with the possibility of chameleons among us. Who knew how many had followed Miguel to Portland?

"I did that while you were checking out the parking lot," Red said.

"So what's the problem?"

"She's not hurt," he said again.

A chill settled over me. Not hurt didn't mean she was all right. "You protecting her from me? Why would you do that?"

"I'm not protecting her from you, Night. I'm just…protecting her. She's afraid."

"Of me?"

He shook his head. "We've just got a little problem."

The sleeping god inside of Faith, the one who'd stirred enough to show her we had trouble on the way. "The Awakened?"

He nodded.

I closed the distance between us slowly, so I could speak softly and have her hear me. "Faith?"

She took a shuddering breath. "Sorry, Night."

"Nothing to be sorry about."

I glanced up at Red.

"The man who came—the straggler?—he would've killed me. I came this close." He lifted a hand, measuring only a slip of space between his thumb and forefinger. "I yelled at Faith to run. She wouldn't go. She went after the guy instead."

I stared at him. My little girl had attacked an Order operative.

"It wasn't me," Faith said.

The part of her that belonged to the god had attacked the operative. "What happened?"

"She…vaporized him," Red said. "One second he was on top of me. The next, he was on fire. Not fire like flames, but burning up from the inside out. He glowed like he was all filled up with gold light. Skin, hair, eyes—everything. And then he started to dissolve right in front of me, Night. He pulled himself upright and ran for the door. He made it as far as the sidewalk."

That explained what I'd seen on my way in. "The walk is scorched."

Faith pressed her head into Red's back, planting it between his shoulder blades. "He was trying to open a door to another place," she said. "A magical door. If he could open it and walk through, maybe he would live. He didn't make it."

A door to the In-Between, judging by the scent I'd caught.

"This is crazy," she said.

Red reached for Faith's hand and wrapped it in his own. "You did good."

"How could that possibly be good?" she asked.

"Saved my life," he said. "Saved your own. That's good in my book."

"That's right," I said. "Faith, why won't you let me see you?"

She pulled her hand from Red's. "What if I hurt you?"

The words felt like a knife to my heart. That she would ever worry about something like that. "That'll never happen," I said.

She raised her head and cocked it to the side, peeking out from behind Red enough that I could see her eyes. Her brown eyes, which weren't brown anymore. They shone gold, with the same color fire that had killed the operative.

"How can you be sure?" she asked.

Looking at the power in those eyes, I couldn't be. Looking at her face, knowing what was in her heart, I had no doubt. "I know you."

She placed a hand on Red's arm, leaning around him a little more. He stepped to the side.

The silver shimmer of her halo was flecked with gold. Not a lot of it, but enough to tell me that something significant had changed with her magic. This morning's revelation aside, what had happened had to have been sudden.

She wore a long, bright purple sweater with a black T-shirt underneath, black leggings, and black riding boots. She'd painted her nails black. Her hands trembled.

The fact that she wasn't curled up on the ground in shock surprised me. I felt grateful as hell for her resilience, for whatever powers had her back, and for Red and the way he watched over her.

I held out my arms. Faith rushed into them.

I drew her close and held her tight, breathing in the scent of her. She still felt the same, albeit more cracked open and easy to read than any sixteen-year-old wanted to be.

She spoke low in my ear. "What the hell is happening, Night?"

I wished I had an answer. I kissed the top of Faith's head. "I don't know. But I'm going to find out."

She pulled away from me a little. "We."

The gold had faded from her pupils, leaving only a gilded rim around the edges. Her eyes, but not her eyes. I recognized the determination in them, however. I'd hadn't been able to keep her out of the heart of things last time we'd had a situation. She'd ended up in deep. Trying to hold her back again was likely to have the same result—or worse.

"We," I said.

Red sighed. "I need to get cleaned up. We need to close up shop for the next few days and head over to the Watcher's house."

I nodded at him, then looked at Faith. "You want to splash some cold water on your face?"

"For real," she said, and stepped around me to make her way back inside.

Red and I watched each other, waiting for the click of the bathroom door closing before either of us said a word.

When the sound finally came, he spoke first. "Jesus."

I rubbed my eyes with the heels of my hands, then brushed the hair away from my face.

"She knew before I did," he said. "Before you'd even finished telling me to get us out of here, Night."

"She knew, or the god inside her?" I asked.

He considered the question, his brows traveling all the way to his hairline and back again. "The lines are blurred."

Faith's magic allowed her to talk with gods, to hear what they said to her. Did she have a way to know which thoughts and feelings belonged strictly to her, and which came from the gods? Or, in this case, the Awakened?

Faith had been in the dark for so long about who I'd been and how she'd come to live with me. We'd been on the run from the Order all of that time. Because using her magic would have drawn unwanted attention, I'd never taught her how to use it properly. No guidelines, no if-this-then-that. Whatever she'd learned had been through trial and error. The problem was that with magic, error could have extreme consequences.

We'd just begun working on the basics, like the divination she and her friends had done last night. The one that had brought us what little warning we'd had this time.

"She needs more training," I said.

He set his hands on his hips. "Yeah, she does."

"It should be a priority."

"Sure. What we can teach her in the thirty days—or thirty minutes—between mortal threats."

That was what it had come to. I sighed. An unfamiliar feeling crept in, taking shallow root in the bowl of my belly. It took me a moment to name it.

Helplessness.

Something I hadn't felt since I'd been a child, back when Red had been the boy next door and I'd been at the mercy of people more concerned with whether my magic had come from the Devil than the fact that I'd been a confused, scared little girl who only needed love and patience.

I'd learned long since how to take control. How to be the decision maker. How to pivot on a dime when circumstances thwarted my plans. I knew from contingencies, and perseverance, and craft and skill.

I no longer knew how to be helpless.

I felt Red's eyes on me, studying me. I met his gaze.

The corners of his mouth turned down. "Night, I thought that was it. When that chameleon came at me, I thought he'd go straight through me to Faith. I thought—"

I stepped into him. He pulled me close. I let his body and his halo envelop me. The grass and earth grounded me in the here and now. It gave me strength I didn't know I needed. I did my best to give that strength to him as well.

"It wasn't the end," I said. "It won't be."

He glanced down at me, lifting my chin so that he could see my face, and I could see his. "You can't make that promise, but you can do something for me."

I waited.

"Faith's not the only one who needs training."

"Your magic is solid," I said.

"My magic isn't tactical," he said. "It's information gathering. I'm good with it, yeah. And I'm strong enough physically. But I've never had to learn how to fight the way you and Sunday do. I've never wanted to, honestly. But I think I need that now."

I couldn't argue with his logic. In fact, I should've beaten him to the punch with it. I should've insisted he get started during the month of relative peace we'd had. I hadn't done that because he'd been coming to terms with my past, and what we had between us was so new. He'd had to figure out for himself whether he could deal with me as I was, and whether he wanted to stick around to help with the trouble on the way.

I drew in a shaky breath. If Red had gone all-in, then he'd weighed the terrible things I'd done and the current and future danger against possibility, and possibility had won out. That meant everything in the world to me. But in for the possibility meant in for the blood and tears, too—the blood on his face and in his hair. The tears that he hadn't let fall, but that I could feel hovering just below the surface.

"All right," I said.

He nodded. "Let's get this place locked up."

I motioned with my head for him to head inside first. After he'd gone, I plucked the phone from my back pocket. I had a text—not from Sunday, asking for a report. From Addie, our local Watcher.

Need you.

That was all.

Watchers shouldn't need their sworn enemies, even those with whom they'd sworn a truce. Watchers supposedly descended from the time before Noah and his ark and the big, Biblical flood—supposedly descended from the mating of humans with the fallen angels called Nephilim.

They kept tabs on people who carried magic, chronicling their activities and monitoring threats. If a threat became imminent, they worked with local magical law enforcement to eliminate the problem. On rare occasions, they even contracted with the Order to hit those magic users they believed too dangerous to be allowed to come into their power.

Our local Watchers consisted of two people. Jess, who was a friend of Faith's and a Watcher-in-training, and her aunt, Addie, who was in her late fifties and had been around the block a time or two. Addie had entered a rare contract with the Order, once upon a time. The person she considered too dangerous to come into their power had been me.

Addie had put out the original hit on me, the one during which an Order operative had tried to kill me and taken out my parents instead. I hadn't forgiven her, and I sure as hell hadn't forgotten. Our relationship was complicated. We'd kept the uneasy truce between us for the last month, since the Angel had come to town.

If Addie needed me—that could not be good. I frowned.

Red had gone to grab a change of clothes from his locker and take a quick shower. A wise choice, given how bloodied and banged up he was. And Faith had retreated to the office, playing games on her phone as if she hadn't fought a life-or-death battle half an hour ago. I could see her from where I stood through the small window. It helped me breathe easier.

I texted Addie back. *On our way in 20.* Then I dialed Sunday's number.

She picked up on the first ring.

"Well?" she said.

"Red's a little banged up."

"Faith?"

I laid out the details for her.

"That's a feature, Night. Not a bug."

"For whom?" I asked.

She sighed. She didn't say any of the things she could have, like how having a god on our side was a good thing. She was thinking it, though. I didn't have to magic my way into her mind to know that.

"What's up with our prisoner?" I asked.

"Worse for wear. He's out and ready for transport."

"Where's he going?"

"Addie's," she said. "The old lady called me. Said she wanted us over there and wouldn't take no for an answer. Said she had containment for Miguel—me, too, if I didn't behave myself. You know how she hates me."

"Not any more than she hates me," I said. "She summoned me, too."

"Shit," she said. "Which do you think it's about—Miguel or Faith?"

"Both," I said. But trouble usually came in threes. I didn't want to ask about a third problem. I didn't want to double dare the Universe to give us one.

"Miguel tell you anything new?" I asked.

A hint of frustration colored her voice. "Not a damn word."

Not surprising. "Addie's?"

"Yep," she said. "See you there."

I tucked the phone back into my pocket, focusing on the weight of my feet on the concrete. It felt normal, like my own experience of gravity. The smell of sulfur lingered just a bit, but it, too, was on its way out.

I turned over the idea—and the feeling—of helplessness in my mind. When I'd been with the Order, I'd had one thing to face and one thing only: do my job. The consequences of failure were severe, and final. After Faith and I had gone on the run, I'd had her to care for, to worry about, to protect. She'd been my only focus. My only reason.

Red was something else.

I'd been wrong to think of what we'd been doing together as light-hearted. Whatever it was, we weren't playing.

I didn't know how to feel about that.

The breeze lifted my hair off my shoulders, sliding across my skin like cool water. The afternoon had traveled on a bit, enough for evening to shoulder its way in. The temperature had dropped a couple of degrees since I'd arrived. The forecast called for a cold, clear night, and maybe some snow in a couple of days.

Very bad timing. Portland and snow didn't mix all that well.

I walked back into the gym, moving from the hard concrete of the dock onto the soft spring of the mats, keeping eyes on the outside, the unknown. I reached overhead to grab hold of the handle at the bottom of the garage door and wrapped my fingers around it, hanging there for a good minute. I gave the back lot with its waving weeds and pockmarked asphalt and the street beyond a last, lingering look. Everything seemed fine to both my eyes and my magical senses. Even so, I felt another prickling at the nape of my neck, hackles threatening to rise.

The information wasn't entirely useless. I'd remain on alert at an instinctual level if nothing else. That would make it harder for someone to get the drop on me—on us. But that was all it was for now. I couldn't fight what I couldn't sense.

Just like I couldn't fight the meltdown that would come for Faith before too long. She was safe, for now. She'd survived the chameleon attack. She'd saved Red's life. She'd also killed a man.

I'd known what that was like at her age, but I'd had one hundred percent of the innocence trained out of me by then, and I'd been taught to kill. Doing what I'd been honed to do had literally destroyed my soul. The one I had left, well, it had been built of the remnants of the souls of people I'd assassinated. I didn't know how. I only knew that I didn't deserve it.

Faith wasn't like me. She still held onto some innocence and gentleness. She'd handled finding out about my past with a remarkable amount of grace, but it didn't rest easy with her. How would she feel after the shock wore off?

I took a deep breath and pulled down the door on the exhale. The door flowed easy on its tracks, its bottom edge hitting with a metal-on-concrete ring that reverberated against the gym's walls and in the depths of my bones.

After the sound faded, I had exactly thirty seconds of peace and calm. Then someone banged on the front door.

Unlikely that anyone with bad intent would've taken the time to knock, but it wasn't unheard of.

I called out to Faith. "Stay put! I got this!"

She didn't listen, even after everything that had happened. In fact, she raced out of Red's office and up the stairs so fast, it was a miracle she didn't trip over her own feet. I ran after her, knowing that if whoever had knocked meant her harm, I'd be too late to stop it.

I heard the door open. The electronic bell chimed. I bounded the stairs in time to see who'd come.

Just one person, and not anyone dangerous to me or mine. He looked at home in the gym because he came here all the time, especially to my 6:00 a.m. weekday classes. He sometimes left his sweaty socks behind in the cubbies. He liked to sit on the man-eating sofa and read on his phone.

Ben Patterson, one of Faith's group of magical friends. He was her age, but he'd already developed a nice set of worry lines across his forehead that made him seem older. He had an unusually deep voice and wary brown eyes that helped with that impression.

I could only see one of his eyes. His long, brown hair and even longer bangs hid the other. He had a thin nose, a meticulously groomed soul patch, and a halo that might as well have been a gray stone wall.

He was a shield. As in, his magic formed a shield against all other magic.

No magic I'd seen so far had been able to penetrate his protections. He could shield himself completely, and he could shield one or two others if they stood beside him. He'd worked hard on that in the last month. His life, and the lives of people he cared about, depended on it.

Today, he'd dressed the same color as his halo. Everything gray, from his boots and jeans to his sweater and hooded coat beaded with rain.

Faith had locked the door behind him. He'd wrapped a hand around her arm, the other hand reaching to open the door. He wanted to leave. Faith wanted to stay.

"Hey," I said.

Ben let go of Faith and turned slowly on his heel. With a toss of his head, he cleared the bangs from his eyes. He met my gaze and waved. "Hey, Night."

"What's going on?" I asked.

"It's not what it looks like," he said.

Not the first time I'd heard that from him. "What does it look like?"

"Like I was trying to take Faith out of here. I mean, why would I do that?"

"I'd love to know," I said. "Let's start at the beginning: what are you doing here? You're supposed to be with the others at Addie's, waiting for us."

"You're late," he said.

I folded my arms across my chest. "Obvious. Pick another choice."

He bit his bottom lip. "There's a problem."

"Addie texted about that."

"This would be a different problem. One she doesn't know about it," he said. "Yet."

"We're all full up on problems right now," I said. "Starting with the fact that I need to look at you. With my magic."

"Right," he said. "Red checked earlier."

"That was then," I said.

His eyes widened. "It feels wrong. No, that's not the right word. It hurts."

"Sorry," I said. "I wouldn't ask if it wasn't necessary."

He took a deep breath and slowly opened a rift in his gray halo. It came apart the way two magnets would—with a lot of effort and strain. I slipped in through the open space and slid into his memory, looking for a piece of Ben that no one else could know. I found it in the memory of a starry July 4th night with his dad on the Oregon coast.

He gasped.

His father had been around more then. They'd walked on the beach that night and talked about important things, and—I withdrew before I dove too deeply. I had what I needed.

He leaned against the door for support as his halo closed again. "Could you not do that again?"

"No promises."

"That's too bad." He studied his boots.

"It is," I said. "So, what are you doing here?"

He glanced up at me, his lips pressed into a thin line.

He shoved his hands into his front pockets. "We might have asked a question about the Awakened during the divination last night," he said. "The cards might've told us that Faith had to be careful using her magic if she wanted to keep the Awakened, well, asleep. We're all linked enough through our magic to know if something bad happens. I felt something bad."

"So you were here to check on her?" I asked.

He nodded.

Behind us, the door to the shower room opened.

"Red?" Ben asked.

I nodded.

"Hey!" Ben called.

Red walked to the foot of the stairs and glanced up at us. He wore a fresh white T-shirt, a pair of faded blue jeans, and his dark blue sneakers. He'd draped his wet bath towel around his neck.

He marked Ben's presence with narrowed eyes. "What now?"

"Fill you in on the way to Addie's," I said. "Faith, grab your stuff."

She headed back down the stairs, into the office, her footfalls heavy. Red stepped out of her way and let her pass, then followed her. He had things to shut off or down. Best he get that done right now. We needed to be on our way.

I met Ben's gaze and held it. I lowered my voice. "Where were you taking her?"

"My house," he said.

Something was off about the way he said that. I couldn't put my finger on it.

"You walk over?" I asked. He lived only a few blocks away.

He nodded.

"You're riding with me to Addie's," I said. "Faith will go with Red."

He shoved his hands deeper into his pockets. He didn't like it at all, but he did what he was told.

He didn't say a single word on the two-mile drive to Addie's place. I kept the radio off, leaving us nothing except the intermittent swish of the windshield wipers and the weight of the uncomfortable silence as we headed south past restaurants and coffee shops to Stark, then east past expensive houses and Laurelhurst Park, where tall Douglas firs guarded the walking trails and the playground.

By the time I parked in front of the house, he held himself rigid in his seat. He reached to unbuckle his seatbelt, lifting his chin to point toward the white Mustang parked in front of us.

"Is that Sunday's car?" he asked.

"Yeah," I said. "You got a good reason for keeping whatever it is to yourself?"

"I do. I know it's frustrating, Night."

I laughed. "That's not the word I'd use."

"Promise not to kill me," he said, as if he were joking. But the jest didn't reach his eyes. "Also, promise that Sunday won't kill me."

I could only speak for myself. Sunday kept her own code. "Promise not to take it too far. We're in deep shit again, Ben."

The Awakened. The chameleon—my long-lost childhood crush, Miguel. It was a lot, and I didn't know how to navigate it yet.

Ben let go of the buckle and allowed the seatbelt to roll back home. He reached out a hand for me to take. "I promise."

We shook on it, making an old-fashioned deal. It struck me as ridiculous, given the stakes—or it would've, if Ben hadn't been so serious.

The brakes on Red's blue pickup squealed as he pulled up behind us. I checked the rearview mirror as Faith poured herself out of the truck, ankles wobbling as she caught her balance on the curb. Eyes downcast. Shoulders cranked up towards her ears.

Mist began to fall as we climbed the front steps, settling over the tall, steep slope of the yard, coating the bare stalks of lavender and the green, fragrant bushes of rosemary planted on either side. The herbs had been planted for more than one reason. Beauty, sure. But also to serve as magical protection, cleansing everyone who passed through the yard and frightening away anyone stupid enough to come here with bad intent.

People in the neighborhood ought to have known by now not to mess with Addie or her niece, Jess. They were kind enough, and friendly, and nothing about them screamed *magic*, but people with the kind of power they wielded radiated a sense of no-nonsense strength. That in and of itself formed a barrier between them and garden-variety miscreants.

The double-decker, buttercream-yellow house had its own, more serious protections inside.

Christmas lights framed the picture windows on either side of the door. The wide wooden porch sported high rails, and it held two oversized wicker chairs in cheerful red with white cushions and a matching wicker table in between. The big old tuxedo tomcat who usually occupied the place had wandered off, leaving a trail of muddy paw prints in his wake.

I peered in through the closest window. As usual, I saw no one in the living room to the right, or in the dining room to the left. Interior lights off—except for those twinkling on the Christmas tree behind the table. But the room beyond—the kitchen—glowed with light and life.

Addie poked her head through the kitchen door before I could raise my finger to the doorbell. Even from this distance, with wood and glass and magic between us, her halo shone. Like all Watchers, her halo held a piece of the night sky—black velvet tossed with stars. Every time I saw her, in the first moment it flashed blue fire so brightly it blinded. Then the flash faded, and I saw her. Or, in this case, her black hair, pulled into a bun, and her dark skin, dark brown eyes, and silver-rimmed glasses perched on her nose.

She waved to invite us in. The door was open, apparently. She ducked back into the kitchen after I nodded.

I took point, pushing open the door and kicking off my shoes, shoving them into the tangled pile of footwear on the right. There was a coat rack and a shoe stand, but both overflowed. I breathed in the gorgeous, evergreen perfume of the tree, and the mouthwatering scent of chocolate chip cookies fresh from the oven. I wondered who Addie had baked them for.

She had a knack for knowing when someone was on their way over, and just what sort of food spoke to the foundational part of them. The food she prepared touched that person deeply, bringing forth memories of childhood, of comfort, of love. Or if the person had never had those things, the dish Addie made conjured them.

It was a gift. It was also an excellent way to get a visitor to let their guard down and open up, to share things they otherwise might not.

Addie's house was her home, and Jess's, first.

It had its own magic, its own power, that took the form of a spirit. To my magical sight, it took the form of a faint, gold shimmer that brushed across my dark-as-midnight halo first before moving on to the others. It recognized me, and I knew it. Had I been a stranger, and unwanted, it would've thrown me out the door.

But I wasn't a stranger. I was an official guest—as in, Addie had given me and mine guest rights in her home. Any insult or harm to me equaled insult or harm to her. That, along with the house's defenses, made it a safe place, a kind of sacred ground. I still marked the exits I knew about and the sight lines, turning them over in my mind.

Addie called from the kitchen, her voice smoky like my *abuela's* had been. "Hey!"

Red stepped up on my left, along with Faith. He rested a hand on her shoulder—whether for comfort or to prevent her from bolting, I couldn't tell. Maybe a bit of both. He raised his voice to carry into the kitchen. "Hey, yourself."

"Get yourself in here, Mr. Jennings," Addie said. "All of you. We got a situation."

Red glanced at me. "I'm afraid to go in there all of sudden."

Faith shrugged off his hand. "Whatever it is, hanging back won't change it."

"Harsh," he said.

She didn't apologize, but she didn't give him any more crap either. She marched into the kitchen like a condemned woman, as if convinced the situation had to do with her.

I moved to catch up, the guys on my heels, and entered the kitchen a couple of steps behind Faith. The hardwood transitioned to well-traveled tile.

Addie stood beside the stove, a bright yellow oven mitt on her right hand. She wore a flowing charcoal gray top printed with black roses and a faded pair of black jeans. Her feet were bare. She pushed a button on the stovetop, turning off the oven. Two sheet pans lined with steaming-hot cookies rested on the burners. She'd bought a new knife block. It bristled with steel.

"Just in time," she said.

Or last in line. The room was packed with more people than I expected. The kids huddled around the long, worn oak table on the other side of the space.

Jess occupied the seat at one end. She had the same Watcher halo as her Aunt Addie, like a night full of stars. She wore a long, plum T-shirt, black leggings, and pristine white sneakers. She'd twisted her dark, kinky curls into a loose bun on top of her head. Her favorite gold hoops dangled from her ears. All five feet of her seemed coiled, ready to spring. She looked at me as if I were her salvation.

From what? I asked the question with my eyes.

She pressed her lips into a thin line. She wasn't telling. Not in her out-loud voice, anyway.

Corey perched on the edge of the chair beside Jess's, her elbows planted on the tabletop as she studied her painted black fingernails. A fire-engine-red bob framed her heart-shaped face. She'd dressed in solidarity with Jess, in a purple-and-black-striped top and skirt set, with purple polka-dotted tights and chunky black Mary Janes. She wore black-and-white skull cameos everywhere—earrings, necklace, rings on every finger. Her halo shone bone-white. Her magic allowed her to speak with ghosts.

Faith made her way to where the girls sat and collapsed into the chair beside Corey's.

Corey looked at Faith from the corner of her eye. Then she leaned in to whisper in Faith's ear, the words too faint for me to pick up.

"Before you ask, Night," Addie said, "Sunday and your prisoner are in my basement, in the temple space. It's magically reinforced, so we're all right for now."

"Thanks," I said.

"I'm all about the détente." She turned an eye toward the back door, which was situated between the table where the girls sat and the sink with its garden window and riot of starter herbs in tiny clay pots. She looked at that door as if it were the door to Hell.

Footsteps behind me signaled that Ben and Red had caught up. Ben didn't come in, though. He hovered on the other side of the threshold, pacing in three-step arcs as if he couldn't make up his mind whether to stay or go.

Red went around him, moving to stand at my back. He rested his hands on my hips. "What's the situation?" he asked.

Addie stripped the pot holder off of her hand and tossed it across the stovetop and onto the counter. "It—he—is outside making a phone call. He probably won't be out there long. His name is Shadow."

"What kind of name is that?" Red asked.

"A very old one," Addie said. "It's not even a name, really. It's a title."

I'd never heard of him, but that didn't mean anything. There were plenty of big, bad things in the world I didn't know about, and I was all right with that. The title thing, though—that gave me pause. Something we'd covered in passing during our early training in the Order. The old, pre-Christian gods often had names that were titles. They fulfilled a purpose in the world. That purpose was their end-all, be-all.

"How old is he?" I asked.

Addie turned her back toward the stove and leaned against the door handle. She met my gaze. She pursed her lips for a quick second, then papered over the gesture with a mask of tolerance. "He's the oldest," she said.

"The oldest what?" I asked.

"Watcher."

Red pulled away from me, sidestepping to get a clearer look at Addie, and a better sight line on the backdoor. "Your boss?"

Her voice softened a little. She liked Red. "Well yes, he is, now you mention it. As if I like being reminded of that in my own home."

Red held up his hands. "Sorry."

"Just don't lie to the man," she said.

"Is he a man?" Red asked.

Good question. Addie and Jess were Watchers, but they looked human, and as far as I could tell, they mostly were. A Watcher that ancient, though?

Addie waved off the question. "You know what I mean."

"Actually, no," Red said.

The handle on the back door turned and the hinges complained. The sun was on its way down, the last rays pouring through pinholes in the clouds, backlighting the being who stood framed in the doorway. He had skin the color of alabaster, and mist-damp hair so blond it might as well have been white. He had thick, long lashes and deep blue eyes—but no pupils. They were just a solid, disturbing cobalt blue.

He wore a white button-down shirt with the sleeves rolled up, tan hiking pants, and dark brown hikers—no coat or other concession to the weather. He smelled like ozone, as if lightning had just struck nearby. He had the Watcher halo, same as Jess and Addie, but his burned with the kind of explosive, starry fire that put me in mind of supernovas.

His voice dipped into baritone, with an undercurrent of thunder. "Night."

"Shadow," I said.

"Like cousins," he said.

"Only I'm not descended from angels."

"Really?" He came inside and shut the door behind him, hanging on to the knob. "Don't those assholes at the Order teach you anything?"

I stared at him. I didn't know whether it was the incongruity of someone like him spouting the word *assholes*, or what he'd actually said. "Come again?"

"Where do you think magic comes from?" he asked.

"I've never given it much thought. Never had the luxury."

I hadn't considered it at all—not since I'd been little and vulnerable, and hadn't been able to understand how people who were supposed to love and protect me could hate me so much. Since then, magic had been a constant. A reality to deal with, to take advantage of, to use. Magic was a survival tool for me and the people I loved.

"All magic comes from angels," Shadow said.

Maybe that was true. Maybe it was just self-serving. "The fallen angels in your bloodline?"

He shook his head. "All of them."

Faith spoke softly from her seat at the table. "What does that mean?"

A hush settled over us as we waited for Shadow to choose his words.

"Your power is destiny. You were born to play a part in whether the world lives or dies," he said. "Magic can save the world. Or destroy it."

CHAPTER 5

S HADOW'S WORDS FELL like boulders into a still pool. For a moment, silence descended again. Everyone seemed to go still: Shadow in front of the back door, one hand still on the knob. The three girls at the long, worn table. Addie, leaning against the oven door handle. I couldn't hear Red's breathing even though he stood right beside me, but I did hear the lack of nervous footfalls outside the kitchen, because Ben had quit pacing.

In the time it took me to count to three, the stillness folded in on itself the way water seemed to compress before it exploded outward. When the spell broke, the ripples were violent and immediate.

Faith rose from her seat so fast, she upended the chair. It hit the wall behind her with a loud crack. She planted her palms on the kitchen table, fingertips digging into the wood. The gold streaks in her brown eyes—the light that reflected the presence of the Awakened—multiplied in the space of seconds.

Over by the stove, Addie stiffened.

I closed the distance to Faith in two long strides, but the table separated us, so I couldn't stop her when she moved to stand toe-to-toe with Shadow. Her hands curled into fists at her sides. She stepped back with her right foot and put all of her weight behind a punch that clocked the oldest Watcher in the right cheekbone.

He didn't react at all, his expression flat and hard.

I moved around the table, ready to pull Faith away from Shadow. Ready to step between them.

"Why are you here?" Faith asked. "Why now? You're going off about all of this existential bullshit while we've got chameleons coming into our places, trying to kill us. You're talking to my mom as if you know her. You don't know her at all. What do you even want here?"

"I'm here now because right now it's not too late," he said. "The forces in the great apocalyptic fight are gathering, but the battle lines aren't set. You, for instance, are still you. The god hasn't yet taken over."

Faith shoveled sarcasm at him. "Oh. So you're here to help?"

"I'm here to make sure that everything happens as it has been foretold."

"Oh, great," she said. "Did you do a divination, too? Or is this bigger than that, like a prophecy?"

He nodded at the latter word.

Faith closed on him, nose-to-nose. "We don't want your help."

He smirked. "You don't get a choice."

At the far end of the table, Jess stood up from her seat.

Over by the stove, Addie stiffened. "Down."

She started to argue. "Faith's right. We don't want him here. Why can't you see that?"

"No," Addie said, with a finality that I felt in my own bones, even though it hadn't been directed at me.

Jess didn't sit, but she didn't move, either. She'd looked to me for help earlier. I hadn't known what kind of help to give, or why she'd needed it.

Shadow cocked his head ever so slightly, studying her face. "Sleep now," he said.

I stepped forward to catch her, thinking he'd cast some sort of spell that would knock her out. But she didn't fall, and I understood that he hadn't been talking to her at all. He'd been speaking to the Awakened.

"There," he said. "That's better."

Faith backed away slowly, moving into my arms. She struggled when I wrapped them around her waist until she realized the person holding her was me.

"What did he do?" She tilted her head back.

He'd faded the gold streaks in her eyes. That left me equal parts relieved and angry. "Red, can you help me here?"

"Got, it. Red gathered Faith and took her out of the room.

Which was where I wanted her—anywhere but in front of Shadow. I glued my gaze to Shadow, so I heard more than saw the exodus from the room as the rest of the kids followed Red and Faith.

That left the two Watchers and me.

I narrowed my eyes at Shadow. "What did you do to my daughter?"

"I stopped the god from coming," he said. "It's temporary. I don't know how long it will hold."

"Side effects?"

"None," he said, then amended. "That I'm aware of. I don't do that very often."

"Oh? When was the last time?"

"A thousand years, give or take."

I'm sure he had a good story about that, but I wasn't interested in hearing it right now. I looked him over more carefully than I had when he'd walked through the door. I didn't see much in the way of weakness. Faith's blow hadn't moved him an inch, whether because I'd only trained her in the basics or because he couldn't be moved against his will remained to be seen.

"Don't," he said. "I'm not here to fight."

"Just to stir up more trouble?"

"Trouble is already here," he said.

I'd thought earlier about the way it always showed up in threes. Damn it all.

He titled his head toward the vacated table, aiming to take a seat there. I took a step back, giving him room to move. He picked up the chair Faith had abandoned, righted it, and straddled the seat. "Addie, would it be all right to get a cup of coffee?"

She took so much time answering, I turned to look at her. She kept her expression blank, but her body tensed like a live wire as she set about plugging in the drip coffeemaker on the counter and raiding the freezer for beans.

Her reaction didn't have a damn thing to do with coffee. She was pissed at Shadow. More than that, she was afraid of him.

Shadow gestured to the empty chair across from him. "Night?"

I walked that way, but instead of sitting, wrapped my hands around the top of the chair. I repeated Faith's question. I wouldn't take existential bullshit for an answer. "Why are you here?"

"Because the chameleon is here, and so are you. This is very dangerous. You can't be in the same proximity," he said.

Were we talking about the prospect of Miguel killing me, or the prospect of something much worse? Harm to Faith? To Red? Or was this about the Angel of Death?

Addie finished her setup, pouring water into the coffee maker and flipping on the power. The machine burbled.

She moved along the counter, edging from out of sight to visible from the corner of my eye. She tucked her fingers behind the handle to a drawer. For ease and speed of opening, or from nerves?

I focused again on Shadow. "Go on."

"The Angel of Death," Shadow said.

Door number three. "What about him?"

"With the chameleon so close, you and the Angel are in a precarious position."

"Can Miguel free him?" I asked.

"Not exactly," Shadow said, then hedged. "Maybe."

"Which is it?"

He scooted his chair forward so that he could fold his hands together and rest them on the table. "The Angel was…kept…at the Order, in the In-Between. You know what I'm talking about?"

Kept? Interesting choice of words. "Miguel talked about the In-Between."

Shadow took a deep breath and blew it out slowly. "The chameleons were created to serve the Angel. To protect him."

To serve and protect. An interesting choice of words. "They're his own personal police force?"

"Try his own personal—what do you call it—elite troops."

"Like magical special forces?" I asked.

"Yes," he said.

Miguel's mind had been a trap for me. In human armies, Special Forces went on recon missions. Miguel had reconned me right away. He continued to try, with every word that fell out of his mouth. Playing on the time we'd been terrified, lonely, and friendless except for each other. Playing on whatever young romantic feelings I'd had for him, and the way I'd mourned him when I thought he'd died.

Everything he'd done so far pointed to an assassination—or suicide—mission.

"Is Miguel here to rescue the Angel?" I asked.

"Yes," he said. "Not the way you think. I—we—believe that the chameleon is here to break your hold on the Angel, and to take your place as the Angel's vessel."

"You think Miguel has the power to do that?" I asked.

"We think he was made for no other reason. He needs to die, the sooner the better."

I blinked at Shadow. "When you say 'we,' you mean the Watchers as a whole?"

He nodded.

The Watchers had been raised in their tradition as much as the Order had raised me. They tracked the magical goings-on in their locales, reporting back in their own mysterious hierarchy. It had to be vast, that organization. They served the Angels—or did what they believed might serve them, since to my knowledge they had no real contact with them. Angels didn't spend their time hanging around in the world of mortals.

When I'd first met Addie, she'd told me that her aim, and therefore the aim of all Watchers, was to locate the Angel of Death and pledge her loyalty. Getting on board with the Angel meant making herself useful in ways no one of her kind had been in a very, very long time.

"Where are you in all of this?" I asked. "The Watchers?"

"We're here to see the Angel safe. Right now, that means seeing you safe."

I didn't believe that for a second. If it were true, the Watchers and the chameleons would be on the same side, not at odds. No, the chameleons wanted control of the Angel for their own reasons, and the Watchers wanted control for theirs. They didn't give a crap about me or mine. We were either in the way, or to be manipulated into doing Shadow's bidding.

Even though I kept those thoughts off my face, he had to know he stood on shaky ground with me. I needed to get my people out of here now. In order to do that, I had to play along a little longer.

"And Jess?" I asked. "What's up with her?"

Shadow sat back in his chair, folding his arms across his chest. "That's our business."

I glanced at Addie. I didn't expect her to show anything but solidarity and loyalty to Shadow.

Sure enough, she raised her chin and kept her mouth shut. But her grip on the drawer handle tightened. Jess didn't want what Shadow had in store, and Addie didn't want it either.

I looked at Shadow again. "You talk to Sunday?"

He didn't answer the question. He pushed to his feet. "I have another call to make. If you'll excuse me? I'll just be a few minutes."

I watched him walk right out the back door. He let in a patch of chilled air as he did. The cold set the skin on my arms to gooseflesh.

Addie spoke quickly, as if she had too many words and not enough time to say them. "You have to go. All of you. I was wrong to bring you here."

I pushed away from the table, bristling.

She rushed me, waving her hands to shoo me out of the kitchen, as if I were a kid with her hand caught in the cookie jar. When I didn't move fast enough, she laid hands on me and moved me where she wanted me to go—out of the room and to the right, down a short hall and around a corner, to the door that led to her basement.

I could've stopped her, but I chose not to. Her fast words and her hands on my body were stone-cold fear. I hadn't known her that long, but I'd seen her handle situations that would give another woman heart failure. She hadn't shown fear before. That she did now spoke volumes. It screamed them, even.

"There's a door down there that leads to the outside," she said. "Comes out around the side of the house. I don't think Shadow has seen it yet, but expect trouble just in case. You take all the kids with you."

"Even Jess?" I asked.

"All of them," she said.

I dug my heels in. "What going on here, Addie?"

She put her hands on my shoulders and shook me. "He's calling in the cavalry. He's got you right where he wants you. He'll kill the chameleon and he'll kill Sunday just for existing. And he'll take Jess, because that's what he came to do. That's what they always do—take the young ones and train them into model goddamn Watchers. If you don't bring her with you, he'll take her to ensure my cooperation in getting you close again. Understand?"

I didn't. But I could piece together that Addie had called us all here to get us where Shadow wanted us—under one roof, trusting her, believing she needed our help, and vulnerable because of that. Maybe she'd had second thoughts along the way, but she'd still done it. And now she'd changed her mind.

"You betrayed us," I said.

She nodded.

I didn't need the details. There'd be time for those later, along with retribution. I didn't cage my thoughts. She read them on my face, loud and clear.

"That'll be then," she said. "This is now."

"You come with us," I said.

She shook her head. "If he's got me to deal with, that gives you a head start. I'll be in touch when I can."

Or if she could. What would Shadow do to her once he understood she'd double-crossed him?

I didn't know how powerful Shadow was, exactly, or what he could sense magically. I didn't want to yell and risk drawing Shadow's attention. I didn't want to reach out with my magic, sending a thread to find Red, for the same reason. I looked over my shoulder toward the staircase to the second floor.

"Red—"

"They're not up there," she said. She cocked her head toward the basement.

When I didn't open the door, she did. The staircase was dark. A faint glow shone down on the landing, illuminating a patch of gray carpet. No sound wafted to us. No voices. No footsteps. Nothing. The air felt colder, the chill of winter seeping from the soil through the basement walls. I tasted ice on the back of my tongue.

"Red wouldn't have taken them down there," I said.

"He sees into the heart of people," Addie said, meaning Red's magic. "He saw Shadow and me."

Who they were. Their intentions. Red would've nailed the betrayal in a heartbeat. He hadn't said anything. He hadn't so much as given me a sign. But I hadn't been looking his way. And he couldn't very well have opened his mouth without giving the game away.

I gave Addie a hard look, face and body language and halo, searching for any lie in her. I saw none, but what I did see felt like a fist closing around my heart.

"Your halo," I said. "The stars are winking out."

"Shadow knows what's up. Go now."

Shit. "He can alter your magic?"

"He can remove me from the chain," she said. "Excommunicate me. So much of our power comes from that connection. Without it, we're defenseless."

I stared at her. "Just like that?"

"Just like that," she said. "Now, get. I need whatever juice I've got left to hold him off."

She opened the basement door and pushed me in—not hard

enough to shove me down the stairs, but with enough force to move me out of the way. She shut the door in my face, sealing me in with the dark and cold.

Before I could draw another breath, the edges lit up with blue fire that burst through seams in flaming rays.

Instinct moved my feet. I backpedaled to the very edge of the top step, reaching for the handrails on either side to catch my balance.

She'd thrown magic at the door to hide it or lock it or both. Her footfalls sounded on the hardwood as she walked back to the kitchen to face Shadow.

Could I break through her magic? Break down the door? If I did it fast enough, could I get to her and drag her out of here with us? Or would I only be running into Shadow's arms? Why would I even consider helping her after she'd set a snare for us?

Addie was fully prepared to sacrifice herself to keep the rest of us safe—or maybe just Jess. The girl was everything to Addie. Addie wanted us out of here. She wanted her niece safe.

Addie could've drawn me in closer instead of sending me away. She could've laid a trap in her own house for me and let Red and the rest get away, giving her boss most of what he wanted. She could've saved her own ass.

She'd made a different choice.

Whatever I could do for her, I didn't think I could save her—not without making her sacrifice meaningless.

I turned and launched myself down the stairs, planting my fore-arms on the rails and sliding down in seconds, landing with a soft *whump* in the glow at the bottom, the carpet absorbing a bit of shock and sound. Strong arms wrapped around my midsection and dragged me into the dark.

My arms were pinned. I had no reach to the floor and little space to move my legs. I threw my head back, drawing a tight breath, preparing to head butt whoever had grabbed me. My next breath tasted of amber and vanilla.

Sunday.

A wave of magic assaulted my senses: a silence that swallowed every other sound, a flash of white light that blinded. Then as quickly as the attack had come on, it subsided.

Sunday set me down in a patch of low light—the shine from a flashlight whose batteries had seen better days, which provided the glow at the foot of the stairs. The floor underfoot felt hard and slick. No longer carpet, but concrete.

I whispered through gritted teeth. "What the fuck, Sunday?"

"Landing's not magically shielded," she said. "Needed you over here and I didn't want to take the time to explain."

"Red and the kids?"

"Gone already. They took his truck and my car."

Which left my car out front. An obvious ambush point. "We should leave on foot."

"Agreed," she said. "Only one problem with that."

Miguel.

We couldn't carry an unconscious, full-grown man around in public. We also couldn't wake him up and walk around with him handcuffed. That left only one choice—one I wasn't ready to make. Sunday might already have made it, though.

I couldn't see Miguel from my vantage. I could only see Sunday's face.

"Did you kill him?" I held my breath.

She shook her head. "Not yet."

Relief that Miguel still lived surged through me. I liked it even less than my instinctive desire to help Addie.

"We're gonna need him," I said. "The Watcher was adamant that he ought to die."

She followed my train of thought seamlessly. "That makes him a potential key to what the Watcher is up to."

She let go of me and led the way to the lawn chair that sat just outside the wan circle of light the flashlight provided. Easy-to-rip, green-and-white woven strips in the back and seat. Flimsy aluminum arms and legs. She'd zip-tied Miguel's wrists and ankles to this one, just like the last.

His head lolled to the left, his face difficult to see in the low light.

Even so, the discoloration around his eyes and mouth from punches Sunday had thrown showed up loud and clear. The front of his shirt was still damp from the water she'd used on him. Dried blood stained the tips of his nails.

His breathing came long and steady. He seemed unconscious. His purple bruise of a halo held a vibrancy that told me Sunday's knockout had worn off, though.

I squatted low, resting my forearms on my thighs. "Cut out the act and listen."

At that, he lifted his head and met my gaze. I laid out the situation.

He took in every word. "So either you slit my throat right here, or we're in this together for now."

I nodded.

"The enemy of my enemy," he said.

Sunday pulled her knife and exposed the blade. "Smart man."

He turned his gaze toward the stairs while we cut his bonds. "Your friend? She's down. Knocked out."

"How can you possibly know that?" I asked.

"They've got angel blood," he said. "I can't feel everything that's happening, but I can get a general read."

"Where's the other Watcher?" I asked.

"Upstairs, outside the basement door, breaking your friend's magic. He's good and he's fast."

I sliced through the last zip tie and hauled him to his feet. He flexed his wrists, giving me a quick glimpse of his palms and the scabbed half-moons his nails had made during the worst that Sunday had done to him.

I turned him around and pushed him toward the side door. "Move."

His ankles gave out a couple of times on our way across the basement, his wool hiking socks slipping on the concrete floor. Sunday caught him both times. I turned my gaze toward the staircase to watch for Shadow, backpedaling behind Sunday and Miguel as quickly as I could.

We streamed through the side door and out onto a narrow stone path between the house and the chain-link fence. The water on the path soaked through our socks. The drizzle falling from the sky had become hard-core rain.

"Hurry," I hissed.

Sunday dug in and turned on the speed, leading us down the stone path between the house and the chain-link fence. She hopped the front gate in one fluid movement that Miguel couldn't duplicate, though he did his best. I vaulted the fence last, checking over my shoulder for Shadow and surprised as hell he hadn't followed. The steep slope of the yard with the rosemary and lavender taking the place of grass should've acted as a hazard, especially since we'd left our shoes behind. Instead, the plants seemed to steer us around roots and rocks.

No one waited by my car, so whatever ambush Shadow had planned, it wouldn't be physical, only magical.

We hit the sidewalk at speed and kept moving.

"We can only travel on foot for so long in this weather," Sunday said. "No coats. No shoes. Soaked to the skin. Hypothermia waiting to happen."

"We're not taking any of the cars around here," Miguel said. "There's Enochian words etched into the hoods—all of them."

Enochian. Angelic language.

Sunday led us south at the first opportunity, toward Hawthorne, where there would be more people and we might blend in—or at least find a doorway to duck into without drawing a ton of suspicion.

I glanced over my shoulder every few seconds, but no one followed.

"Why aren't they on top of us already?" Sunday asked.

Miguel kept pace with us, but the air around him stilled, as if he'd sent his spirit walking temporarily. He blinked a moment later. "The other Watcher is also down. Something in your friend's magic at the basement door backfired on him. He's out cold. No idea for how long, though."

I'd take good news where we could get it. "I'm surprised at you."

"That I haven't taken off already?" he asked.

I nodded.

"I thought about it," he said. "But the ancient Watcher might be able to track me, and if he does, better I'm not on my own. Two, if the chameleons are tracking me, better that they think I'm still on mission, not captured. And then there's the bonus."

"Enlighten us," Sunday said.

"I missed you two."

"Sure you did," she said. "I mean, what's a little torture between friends?"

"I wouldn't know," he said. "I don't have any friends."

Sunday rolled her eyes. "I'm supposed to feel sorry for you?"

I didn't care who felt sorry for whom. I only cared that the cavalry Addie had mentioned could swoop down on us at any minute. And that I had no idea where Red had taken the kids, or whether they were safe. And that because Addie had sold us out to Shadow, and she knew where we lived and worked, we had no safe place to go to. Nowhere to hide.

I reached for my phone. As I punched in my passcode, it buzzed with an incoming text from Red.

An address in northeast Portland. Nothing else for a hot minute. Then a single word: Dorothy.

As in *The Wizard of Oz*. As in the name of the blond Labrador retriever he'd had as a boy, the one who'd stayed by my side on the worst night of my life.

"Dorothy" was the verification word we'd decided on in case we were ever separated, in trouble, and trying to connect. No imposter would know that word or what it meant. We would never utter it under duress.

I passed the phone to Sunday. She took a look, then pulled out her own phone and called for a ride.

"The Watchers will be tracking us," she said. "It would be better if we could lead them away from the others."

A worthy thought. A smart one, even. At most, we'd draw the Watchers toward us and the others would have a shot at escape. Even worst case, it would split the Watchers' attention—one group would go after Red and the kids, while the rest of them came after us.

"There's just one problem with that," I said.

"No way will Red and the kids run," she said. "Even if Red ordered the others to go—even if he dragged them to hell and back himself to keep them safe—they would find a way to help us."

I nodded. "They think safety is overrated."

"They're sixteen, so of course they think that," Sunday said. "They're only half right, though. Safety's not just overrated."

"It's an illusion," I said.

Twenty-five minutes later, an overly talkative Trailblazers fan of a driver who'd shown to pick us up in his baby blue Prius dropped us off on a quiet cul-de-sac in front of a white house with an enormous, curtained picture window and a yard full of bare, thorny rosebushes. I tipped him twenty in cash on account of the puddled mess we left in his cab.

We moved up the walk as a wary, weary unit, stumbling up the steps to a wide cement porch. On either side of the porch, rain barrels stood guard, taking on trickling streams of icy water from the rain chains that hung from the eaves. Tiny Christmas lights hung nearer to the front door, casting halos of light that made me feel as if we stood inside of a kaleidoscope.

I could see the defenses on the place. Nothing that would draw the eye of any normal human being, or even the curiosity of someone with magic. The shields hugged close to the wood and glass. They gave off no color. No sense of who'd placed them. Which meant that the person who'd placed them was a shield himself.

Ben had done it.

The door to the house opened before we reached it. Red held it open as we filed in, casting a worried glance at Miguel.

"You couldn't have done something else with him?" Red asked.

Sunday shrugged. "As it happens, we need him."

Red closed the door and locked it—two deadbolts and a hinged lock for overkill's sake.

We dragged mud and leaves into the white-tiled entry. Peeling off our wet socks and stepping into the warm, dry living room felt like walking into heaven. If the rest of my wet self dripped all over everything, whoever owned or rented the place would have to live with that.

The house smelled like no one lived there—it had none of the layers that came from frying eggs and sleeping and showering every day. It sported a wood-burning hearth where Red had obviously been in the process of building a fire—the screen had been pulled back and away, and bunch of store-bought cedar logs had been dragged from a big, brand-new basket at the side of the fireplace, the big yellow band that'd held them together sliced open. The red brick mantel held a couple of tarnished pewter candlesticks and a pack of worn playing cards. No art graced the plain, white walls. The furniture consisted of four large navy blue beanbag chairs set in the corners and a worn navy rug.

None of the adults I knew would buy furniture like that.

Sunday pointed at Miguel, then at the beanbag furthest from the door. "Sit."

He eyed the thing skeptically. "If I sit in that thing, you're never getting me out of it."

"Even better," she said.

"Can I at least get a towel?" he asked.

"In a minute," Sunday said. "If there are any."

He screwed up his mouth in protest, but he did what she told him, sinking like a rock into a pool of Styrofoam pebbles. He pulled his long tail of hair over his shoulder, wringing out a ton of water onto the rug.

The living room butted up against the kitchen via a granite-topped bar, sans stools. The kitchen was wide and packed with stainless steel. It had a breakfast nook, too, which had been set up with a card table and folding chairs. I could tell from the glow behind the oven door that something was cooking, but I couldn't smell it yet.

Beyond that, a long hall led back to the bedrooms. The sound of conversation wafted from there. The kids. All of them, thank God.

I turned to look at Red. "You all right?"

He nodded. "You?"

"We got out," I said.

"Addie?"

I shook my head. "She's still with Shadow. I think she's still alive."

He set his hands on his hips and studied the floor for a moment before he looked at me again. "We need to plan."

"At least for the short term," I said. "Exit routes? Points of entry?"

"I'll show you," he said.

Windows in every room except the kitchen and bath, all of them working and locked for now. Two doors, front and back, both steel. No basement. Crawl spaces in the coat closet and the closet in the master bedroom, barricaded. A couple of trees in the backyard, along with the usual trash bins, so not much in the way of cover for an enemy. And all of it—the entire house and yard—under Ben's magical protection.

It was a good short-term solution to a long-term problem.

"Whose place is this?" I asked.

"The kids'," he said.

The kids. Including my daughter. "How'd they get a place of their own? They're sixteen. How'd they do this without us knowing?"

Without *my* knowing.

"Belongs to Ben's cousin," Red said. "They moved out, but they're not ready to sell yet. They'll be staging the house to sell next week, but no one's checking up between now and then. Ben went next door and explained that we're watching the place. Neighbor knows him, so it's not a red flag. No worries there."

So, we'd be invisible to the Watchers, at least for a while. My wired nerves relaxed a hairsbreadth.

"If there's trouble tonight, you take the kids and get out," I said. "Leave the fighting to Sunday and me."

"And Miguel?" Red asked. "He gonna help you, too?"

"His ass is on the line along with ours. He gets out of line, he's dead."

Red mulled that for a moment. "We're not helpless, Night—me, or the kids."

"It's not about that," I said. "I know you can fight."

He mirrored by words. "It's not about *can*. It's about *will*. I'll leave you here if you ask, even if it kills me to do it. I can't control the kids if they're not on board. They're nearly grown, and they've got power in them. Besides, where would we go that the Watchers won't find us?"

He was right. It didn't matter whether I liked it or not. If the Watchers could track us by our shared angel blood, or if they could track Jess because she was a Watcher, running and hiding were off the table.

"We'll do the best we can," I said.

"And tomorrow?"

Either we waited for the Watchers to come to us, or we took the battle to them. "There'll be blood."

He swallowed hard.

I turned toward Sunday. "Can you keep an eye on Miguel?" I asked.

"Ten-four," she said.

Red sighed. "I'll get the fire going. There's two take-n-bake pizzas in the oven. I just put 'em in. There's more in the freezer if we want 'em."

That would do well enough to stem the gnawing in my belly. No breakfast and no lunch plus mayhem had me ready to eat an elephant. "Thanks."

He cocked his head toward the back of the house. "Don't be too hard on 'em."

I flashed him a wry smile and got moving.

They heard me coming. Faith knew my step, even if the others didn't. They'd gathered in the farthest of three bedrooms, which appeared to have housed much younger children, judging from the scratches a bunk bed frame had made on the far wall and the blue-and-white twinkle-star wallpaper border. Whatever else had been there before, the kids had replaced it with brand new, plastic-stinking, full-sized air mattresses laid into the space like pieces of a jigsaw puzzle. The cobbled-together sheet sets gave me a headache just looking at them, mix-and-match Dalmatian spots and basketballs and green-checked flannel. A red banker's lamp set on the floor lit one corner. A badly balanced black floor lamp with a white shade handled the rest of the illumination duties.

To their credit, every single one of the kids met my gaze when I stepped inside. They displayed no shame, no fear. Their posture telegraphed tension—hunched shoulders, hands curled into fists, crossed ankles—but not about me.

The anger I felt at their having done something like this behind our backs—behind my back—what did it mean when the lot of us could've ended up on the street with nowhere to go to ground? Instead, we were warm and dry and we'd have full bellies before long.

Every one of them had made a decision to join this fight. Faith had a deeper knowledge of the risks, having spent years on the run with me, but the others only had an inkling of what they'd volunteered themselves into. They'd taken the possibilities seriously. They'd prepared this place in a month's time while it'd never occurred to Sunday or me that we might need this kind of contingency.

Faith scooted over on her air mattress to make room for me and waited for me to settle. She started to take off her purple sweater, but quit halfway, leaving the sweater arms empty at her sides.

"Thank you for all this," I said, making sure the words touched all of them, especially Ben.

He hugged his knees to his chest. His long hair hid half his face. "You're not still mad that I lied?"

"Sure I am," I said.

"Well, that makes me feel better."

"How's that?"

"It's normal," he said.

"It should be," I said. "Why didn't you trust me enough to tell me about this place?"

He let go of his legs. They slid out long in front of him. He glanced at Jess.

She nodded.

He took a deep breath. "Because we thought we might have to hide Faith."

"From whom?" I asked.

He didn't answer the question. In not responding, he'd spoken as clearly as if he'd shouted my name out loud.

Corey linked her skeleton-cameo be-ringed fingers and pressed her palms into the crown of her head. "It's not like that, Night."

"It's one hundred percent like that," I said. "Now I'm even more pissed."

Jess held up her hands. Her brown eyes held barely contained fire. Her Watcher's halo flashed blue fire that reflected her strength. "No, Night. This wasn't—isn't—about you."

The hell it wasn't. "You're talking about hiding my daughter from me."

"Why would we do that?" she asked. "You want to tell me?"

That question stopped whatever had been about to roll out of my mouth. Jess and the others would only feel the need to keep Faith from me for two reasons. One, they feared that I would hurt her—which was ridiculous. Two, they feared Faith would hurt me. I couldn't imagine that.

But the Angel of Death and the Awakened? I had no idea what they might do.

I turned to look at my daughter. "Did you know any of this?"

She shook her head. "Not until tonight. Not until we got here."

I rested my hands on my thighs. I was afraid that if I didn't, they would start to shake. "Are you okay with it, Faith?"

"No," she said. "I've already told them that. I get it, though."

I did, too. "This really isn't about me. It's about the Angel. And the Awakened."

Jess nodded. "You're both"—she searched for the right word—"incubating something powerful. If I'm guessing, you think you have control over yours, Night, but what if you don't? We know Faith doesn't have a prayer with hers. What happens if something, well, happens?"

Corey picked up where Jess left off. "That chameleon came after you at breakfast, and his backup showed at the gym this afternoon. Who knows who else the Order might've sent. There's a rogue

Watcher at Jess and Addie's house and the breakfast assassin is in the fucking living room."

"Watcher's not rogue." Jess glanced down, playing with the hem of her purple T-shirt. She looked at me through her lashes.

"I know," I said.

She uncrossed her ankles. The floor lamp reflected off the shiny surface of her white sneaks.

Corey dropped her hands to the mattress she sat on, braced her arms, and leaned forward. "My point is, that's a helluva lot of stress."

Faith hugged herself. "It's making things unstable. It's making *me* unstable."

Ben nodded. "We saw your eyes at Addie's. The gold in them. I saw it at the gym, too."

"I don't know what to do about it," Faith said.

"We can start by checking out of the stress," Corey said.

Faith bit her lip. "I don't think that's possible. We can't just pretend none of this is happening."

Jess frowned. "And our place to hide out isn't a hideout anymore."

"No," I said. "But it's what we have and, like I said, I'm grateful for it. We need a plan for tonight, and to regroup in the morning."

"Will we be safe that long?" Corey asked.

Jess met my gaze. "She can't guarantee that."

"You're right," I said. "Sunday's house is the fallback. Y'all know where it is?"

"The Watchers know about it," Jess said.

Of all our places, it still made the most sense. "True, but it's the best alternative we've got for a local place to meet up if we get separated. Addie hasn't been there, so that has to count for something."

"She won't know anything about the protections. I didn't tell her anything." Jess blinked back sudden tears.

Jess didn't trust Addie. That was the only reason not to give her that kind of information.

The only reason I'd found out that Jess and her aunt were Watchers in the first place was because Jess had gone against Addie's wishes and told me. Jess had heard warnings about me, but she'd also gotten to know me, so a lot of what she'd heard didn't hold water. She'd chosen to trust me and, by extension, Sunday.

Fast-forward to the here and now. Jess knew that Addie had been ready to hand her over to Shadow. That the Watchers had an agenda for which Jess didn't have all the details.

I sighed. In the Order, there'd been no such thing as trust, only missions and the threat of violence and death. Out here in the world, it ought to be different. I needed it to be.

"So it's a plan," I said.

The kids nodded.

Jess studied her fingernails, working on a question.

I thought I might know what she wanted to ask. "I'm not sure whether Addie's okay. She risked herself to help me, to get Sunday and Miguel and me out. She asked me to take care of you."

Jess swallowed. "Thanks for not lying to make me feel better."

"Sorry that I can't tell you for sure," I said.

"She's got a lot of power," Jess said.

"She does," I said. "She's strong."

Jess closed her hand into a fist. "I'm going to count on that as much as I can."

I nodded. "We need to count on each other. Can we do that?"

Ben met my gaze. I could see the thoughts turning behind his eyes as he weighed possibilities. I understood that trust could get us all killed. The future would always remain unknowable, even if fortunes or prophecies provided clues. We could never truly know everything about each other. But if we couldn't depend on each other, we'd be lost long before our enemies had a chance to end us.

He leaned forward, reaching for the center of the circle, an invitation for solidarity.

I placed my hand on top of his. One by one, the others did, too.

The blissful, greasy, meaty scent of pepperoni and sausage wafted in through the door. My stomach rumbled.

Jess laughed, granting permission for the others to join in. She led everyone toward the kitchen—everyone except Faith. She stayed right where she sat. I stayed with her.

"Night," she said. "Do you think they were right, getting this place together? The reason they did it?"

I'd already said as much—or that I understood, anyway. She'd heard me. She knew I meant it. "You're asking whether they're right to be worried that I'd hurt you. Or that the Angel would."

She fidgeted. "I don't even want to—it feels awful to ask that."

How had she made it through the day without breaking down? She'd been on the verge at the gym. Now, she seemed to be holding it together. It didn't seem like normal young person resilience, or even magical young person resilience. It couldn't be shock—she'd have gone down by now. Adrenaline? Maybe.

It scared me more than a little.

I didn't want to lie to Faith, or make promises I couldn't keep. I didn't want to treat Faith like a child. Yes, she was my kid. But she was growing up, and doing it much faster than anyone should have to.

"I promise that I'll do everything in my power to make sure that doesn't happen," I said.

"It might not be in your power," she said.

I mulled that over. "I know. It feels awful to say that."

She leaned into me. "What's the rest of the plan?"

"For tonight? Sunday and I will take turns keeping watch. Everyone eats. Everyone sleeps."

"What about Miguel?" she asked.

Good question. "We won't let him run free around here."

"I know," she said. "But what are you gonna do with him?"

The whole "enemy of my enemy" thing would only take us so far. "That depends on him."

She pushed to standing, all awkward knees and elbows. "Pizza's calling."

Out she went, and before I could follow, Sunday and Miguel marched in with paper plates piled high with as many steaming-hot slices as they would hold. Sunday handed me the slices with extra olives.

"Veggies," she said.

I stared at the plate I held, then set it down on the mattress beside me. "Is this where we have that talk about how if Miguel gives his solemn oath that he'll help us, we'll treat him like a friend?"

He kicked the door shut and leaned against it. "Like I'd swear to that."

He downed half of his first slice in one swallow. I wasn't sure he'd even tried to chew it.

"What then?" I asked.

"I will swear to protect you, Night," he said. "I know you'll believe that."

"Because of the Angel." Every goddamn thing that had happened today came down to that.

He saluted me with the remainder of his slice, then took a huge bite.

"And the rest of us?" I asked.

"I'm on board. Besides, the kids remind me of us when we were little."

"They're not us," I said.

He wiped his greasy fingers on his pants. "What are you protecting them from?"

Isn't that obvious?" I asked.

He shook his head.

"Becoming us," I said.

His mouth fell open for a moment. Then he snapped it shut.

"That's more like it," Sunday said. "Shut up and eat. Night, you want to eat in here with us?"

"Hell, no." I stood up, knees cracking, and picked up my cooling pizza.

"We'll take first watch," she said.

We. Not a word I wanted to get used to including a chameleon, or any other Order operative. "Wake me at—"

I stopped the sentence in its tracks. I had no idea what time it was.

"It's six-thirty," Miguel said.

Might as well have been midnight, the way I felt. "Wake me at one."

I left them in the kids' room, stepping into the hall, which ought to have been filled with voices and laughter and inappropriate jokes, with some top-secret planning as the cherry on top. But the kids had gathered in front of a computer screen in the far corner of the living room, watching something with explosions, leaving Red alone in the kitchen amid denuded cheese-dotted, grease-spotted aluminum pans and stained and wadded white paper napkins. Someone had spilled a packet of crushed red pepper on the floor. Someone was going to have spicy feet if they weren't careful.

Red cocked his head, inviting me to join him. He eyed the mostly intact dinner on my plate. "You gonna eat that, or just carry it around?"

I made a clear spot on the counter and set down my plate. "Jesus, Red."

"I know," he said. "You don't eat, it's gonna start affecting how you respond."

I shot him a side-eye glance. "You always know just what to say to a woman."

"I don't know from women," he said. "I know you."

And what mattered to me. I picked up a slice and bit in. The salty sausage and olive combination tasted like heaven. I didn't need any encouragement after that to polish off the contents of my plate, or to pluck leftover bits of cheese and olives from the nearest pan.

He let me be while I ate, not watching me so much as keeping company with his own thoughts.

I licked my fingers. "Not what you signed up for, is it?"

"I had no idea what I was signing up for other than staying with you." He leaned back further, planting his elbows on the counter. "You know, I never stopped thinking about you after the night your parents were killed. I always wondered whether you were alive, where you were, whether you were okay. And then you showed up on my doorstep and I couldn't for the life of me figure out how or why. I know it was an accident, or a coincidence—at least, that's what a lot of people would call it. But I don't believe in those things with the important stuff. So you showed up, and trouble followed, just like the first time. And I didn't care. Foremost thing in my mind was that I didn't want to lose you again, and I'd do whatever it took."

"My past aside?"

"Everyone has a past. Yours is hard to get over—I'll give you that. I hoped we'd have more time before trouble came calling again."

Me, too. I opened my mouth to say so, but he shook his head.

"Let me get all this out first, Night. Like I said, this started out with my not wanting to lose you. But then there's the kids. I love those kids. I can't stand to think about what would happen to them if I tapped out. I know I'm not their savior, and that you and Sunday would do your best, and that those kids are anything but defenseless. But that's not the point. I've never been able to walk away when I'm needed."

We did need him. Could we take on the Order and the Angel—whatever else came—without him? Maybe. Would we be able to win without him? Maybe.

I knew exactly who I was, regardless of my attempts to leave the Order behind. I was an assassin. It was in my blood. Trained into my every muscle. The fact that I had a soul was down to a miracle. That fragments of the souls of my targets had knitted together to form that soul—there was no force in the universe that could explain that. Because of them, I understood the value of life. I understood that the stakes were much bigger than me.

Sunday? Well, Sunday had fewer qualms and greater skills than I did. Her moral compass was seriously bent.

Red had what we didn't and couldn't hope to. He held the center together. He was a do-the-right-thing anchor. He made sure the means justified the end. He was everything we weren't. Everything I wasn't.

I stepped in front of him so neither of us had to look far to meet the other's gaze. "So you're staying."

"It's a little more than that," he said. "This—whatever this is—it's a long haul. Now that I've seen what's going on, I can't close my eyes and pretend that it's all a dream. I'm not wired that way. I'm saying that I'm in, Night. All in."

"With the fight." That was good. Important. Necessary. I nodded.

He bent toward me, close enough that I could feel his breath on my skin. He gripped the edge of the counter with his fingers. "Not just the fight."

I closed my eyes. A shiver started in the soles of my feet, traveling up through my spine all the way to the top of my head. We'd had hardly any time to know each other, to learn each other in the day-to-day. I understood better how he moved through crisis. How he dealt with life-and-death risk. I trusted him without reservation. That was rare enough.

But now he was talking about the thing we'd agreed not to discuss.

"I didn't think you'd go there," I said.

"Is it a problem?"

I looked at him. "No. Just…why now?"

"Because between the time the kids and I ran from Addie's house and the time you showed up here, I felt fucking terrified. Afraid that you were hurt or dead or taken. I worried about it for Faith's sake. That's not what I'm talking about now, though. I'm talking about the thought of losing you. I felt like a coward, not telling you sooner what's on my mind and in my heart."

His words slipped right past the defenses I'd put up against them. I wanted to feel angry. With everything that had happened today, and what could happen tomorrow, I didn't want to talk about how we felt. I didn't want to acknowledge that there was one more thing at stake. One more crucial thing.

What I needed to say felt like a fire inside—the same fire I'd felt this morning, before Red and I had climbed out of bed. I'd wanted him then, but it'd been more than that. So I spoke slowly. I feared that if I didn't, the fire would burn me from the inside out.

CHAPTER 6

"**T**HIS IS IMPOSSIBLE," I said.

Red held my gaze. His eyes filled with hurt that he masked so quickly, I'd have missed it if I hadn't been looking right at him. He tightened his grip on the edge of the kitchen counter until his knuckles bleached.

The mess of emptied pizza pans and spilled condiments seemed to fade. I could hear the crackling of flames in the living room fireplace, along with an explosion and the squeal of tires from the movie the kids were watching out there, but that faded away as well.

Red was all I could see, his grass green and earth. His breath on my face was all I felt. The thump of my own heartbeat and the rush of my blood in my veins were all I heard.

"It's impossible because of the situation, what we're facing. All I wanted was time, which clearly we're not gonna get. I only wanted to figure things out slowly, to understand what I'm feeling."

"Is it about Sunday?" he asked. "The thing you have to sort out?"

I blinked at him.

He knew Sunday and I had been together before. He knew she'd cleaned up my mess the night I'd chosen not to kill Faith, after I'd taken Faith and run. She'd taken out the follow-up team the Order had sent. She'd made sure we were safe.

She'd left the Order and followed me to Portland. She'd done all of it because she loved me.

"No," I said. "Not the way you think. Just listen. Can you do that?"

He didn't answer, but he didn't look away either.

"Sunday is the only person I was ever with before. I loved her the way someone with nothing to lose loves—completely and utterly. She loved me the same way. Somewhere along the line, it wasn't enough. Sunday and I are friends now. We still love each other. Would still do anything for each other."

He shifted his weight from one foot to the other. "This isn't helping."

"She stayed here to fight with us even though there's no chance of rekindling what we had. She did that for love, and if she ever needed me for any reason, no matter how far around the world she was, I'd go. Understand?"

He let out a breath he'd been holding.

My voice trembled. "The reason I've been avoiding talking about us isn't because I don't care enough," I said. "It's because I care too much. I'm no longer the person I used to be—someone with nothing to lose. Now, I have everything to lose, and it scares me to death."

The fire inside of me still burned. I could hardly believe it hadn't scorched me. Surely it would. Any second now.

Red peeled his fingers from the counter's edge and reached up to cup my face in his hands. "You want to run from this?"

"I don't think I can," I said. "It would follow me wherever I'd go."

The wonder I'd seen in his eyes early this morning bloomed again. "Sunday told me she's taking first watch."

I nodded.

"There's an empty bedroom in the back," he said.

The house was full of people in hiding. We weren't yet under siege. We could breathe now, even if it was just for a little while.

I pulled his hands away from my face. I kissed one palm, and then the other.

He slid away from the counter, leading me down the hall, away from the crackling hearth and the movie explosions. We passed Miguel and Sunday on our way as they headed toward the front of the house. Miguel didn't say a word, nor did he do more than glance at either of us.

Sunday hung back—not to talk to me, though she flashed me a quick grin. I left her with Red for a moment, which was all the time she needed to lean into him and pass on a message. She pitched her voice low, but I overheard anyway.

"Don't fuck it up," she said.

And then she moved on her way, leaving Red to catch up with me at the door to the spare room.

I'd expected a bare floor and darkness, but instead saw that someone had left a camping lantern in the corner, and laid out a red blanket on top of the carpet. They'd left us a couple of pillows as well.

"Did you do this?" I asked.

"No," he said.

It had to have been Sunday and Miguel. If that didn't make me feel an awful combination of embarrassed and out of my depth—I didn't want to waste time feeling those things.

I turned into him as he shut the door and turned the tiny lock in the knob. The words I'd meant to say fled the second he gripped my hips and pulled me closer. I wrapped my arms around his neck and drew his lips down to meet mine.

I kissed him with all the urgency I felt inside, tasting salt and green and earth and a tenderness he'd been holding back. He skimmed the sides of my body with his knuckles, moving up and along the curves of my breasts, thumbs sliding across my nipples. I moaned, the sound born deep in my belly.

Then Red's hands moved again, this time pulling at the hem of my shirt, lifting it over my head, and at the clasp of my bra, unhooking and drawing it away, dropping it to the floor. He danced me toward the blanket and lowered us down. He kissed my neck and my breasts, and I melted under his lips and his touch until all I could do was feel.

He made me naked, and I let myself become naked—not only my body, but my heart as well.

The cotton of Red's T-shirt, soft as it was, chafed. I needed to feel his skin on mine. He pulled away long enough to grant my wish, tossing the shirt aside, giving me room to trail a hand from the beautiful sacred heart tattoo that covered his chest down the hard muscle of his stomach, hooking my fingers in the waistband of his jeans.

He looked into my eyes and he saw the fire there. He saw me.

He let me see into him, too, pulling back the curtain of his own defenses, and even the curtain of his magic. As the green and earth parted, something else took its place: the fiery crown of the sacred heart on his chest became a magical fire—a golden flame of devotion and compassion. A fire of the soul.

I met his gaze and held it. He slid off his jeans and boxers, never once glancing away. I opened my legs as he drew close again. He pressed against the wetness between my thighs, teasing. He lowered the rest of his body until there was no space between us, until we lay heart to heart.

He whispered in my ear. "You understand me?"

I thought I did. I wanted to be sure.

I reached for him with my magic. He opened to me, inviting me into his mind. I read in him everything I needed to know.

This wasn't like any other time before. This was lust, but more than that. He was giving all, and hoped for the same in return.

I didn't know how to do what he'd done, how to let him see as deeply into me. I closed my eyes, feeling my way into my own magic, into the moon-glow and tidal pull on the waters of my own halo. I let the soft glow shine forth, and the waves flow and ebb. I opened the depths of the sea beneath. The glitter of the light on the surface. The velvet depths of the dark water beneath.

He gasped.

I opened my eyes just barely and gazed at him through my lashes, afraid of what I would see on his face. What I saw took my breath away.

Love.

He slid inside me then, and we were one in body, mind, and magic. He matched his thrusts to the rhythm of my waves. I fisted my hands in his hair and rode with him in a dance of fire and water. Every move —every breath—made us stronger. Every moment, the magic built between us and around us, the firestorm and the hurricane. I surrendered to the power of it, becoming the water as it rose to meet the sky —and fell.

He closed his mouth over mine as I exploded into a million glittering shards. A heartbeat later, he followed.

I came back slowly, consciousness returning along with the feel of Red's weight on top of me, and the slickness of his sweat, and the pulse of his heart. Steam rose from his skin—and mine. It was more than heat rising into a chilled room. It was power. It was what we'd built together.

He searched my eyes, his voice soft. "You with me here?"

"Yes," I said. "Yes, I am."

"How did we do that?" he asked.

"The way our magic wove together," I said. "I don't know."

He nodded. "Has that ever happened to you before?"

"No. You?"

"Never," he said.

"I never thought something like that was even possible."

"We should try again." He gave me a lopsided grin.

I brushed the shaggy, damp hair away from his face. "You know, when you smile like that, your mustache smiles, too."

He laughed.

I laughed, too. It started out gentle. I didn't mean for it to go on, and what I'd said wasn't all that funny, but the sound sang inside of me and something I'd held together with pain and fear broke open. I laughed until my belly hurt. Until I could hardly breathe, and tears streamed from the corners of my eyes.

"Wow," Red said. "When was the last time you did that?"

"Laughed?"

He shook his head. "Got silly."

I tried to remember. My forehead knotted with wrinkles.

Red smoothed them out with his fingertips. He planted a kiss on my brow, then rolled onto his side. I curled into him, listening to his breathing deepen. I could sense that he was thinking, but I couldn't read his thoughts. The joining of our magic had slipped.

"What?" I asked.

"You can't recall, can you?"

I shook my head.

"That's got to change," he said. "You worry too much."

"I'm not tilting at windmills," I said. "The stuff I worry about is real. And I wouldn't call it that, exactly. It's more like planning. Strategizing."

"It's endless."

"No," I said. But how could I be sure there would be an end when the forces arrayed against us were so many, and the hits kept on coming?

"Can I ask you something, Night?"

His tone had me pushing up on one elbow, resting my head in my hand. I wanted to see his face. I waited.

"If you're always planning, always fighting—what are you fighting for?" he asked.

That was an easy ask, an easy answer. "To keep Faith safe. To keep all of us safe. And...." I trailed off, because I saw the rabbit hole open up in front of me.

There was also *to save the world.*

Which sounded arrogant and stupid. And something I had to do.

Red followed my train of thought without my having to spell it out. Maybe because he knew me. Maybe because the combination of our magic hadn't slipped as much as I thought.

"You want to save everybody," he said. "What are you saving them for? What kind of world do you want for them?"

One where we didn't have to look over our shoulder all the time. One where safety didn't depend on constant vigilance. Where laughter wasn't a rare occurrence, and joy wasn't a foreign feeling.

I'd never lived in a world like that, but it was the kind of world I wanted.

"Jesus, Red."

"I know," he said. "Just think about it. That's all I'm asking."

I lowered my head to his chest. He pulled me close. I turned the questions over in my mind until exhaustion took me over and I slipped deep into sleep and dream.

I expected something peaceful, something crafted from the sound of Red's heartbeat and even breathing, from the solidness of him. Or something troubled, as I considered what he'd asked, and all the ways in which I walked in the world as an outcast, as a creature apart from normal human things.

Magic. Training. Blood on my hands. The strange shape of my soul. The Angel of Death locked inside of me.

I found myself in the living room of the house. I wasn't sleepwalking; I still sensed my body tangled with Red's in the back bedroom. I was definitely dreaming.

The corner where the kids had watched their movie earlier was quiet now, occupied by Ben, who slept with his arms straight out and his legs thrown wide, taking up as much space as humanly possible, and Jess, curled into a ball and pressed into his side. Best friends, those two. And they had feelings for each other, clear as day.

Faith and Corey had gone to bed properly, in the room full of air mattresses. I couldn't see them from where my dreaming self stood, but I could feel them. They were in the house, and safe, and that was what mattered.

The scent of grease and pepperoni still hung in the air, but the empty pans had been tossed into a white plastic trash bag that sat at the far end of the kitchen. The counters and floor had been wiped down. Sunday or Miguel had brewed a pot of drip coffee and drunk most of it. The rest had begun to congeal in the bottom of the glass carafe, but not yet to burn.

Sunday sat in in a beanbag that she'd dragged in front of the fireplace, where the flames cracked and popped. She'd let her blond curls down and tucked the sides behind her ears. She worried at the scar on her lip the way a person might worry at a memory they couldn't shake. She'd stretched her legs out in front of her, toes digging into the pile of the rug, and allowed the fire to mesmerize her—or she cultivated that appearance.

But the fire in her halo burned bright. She watched Miguel from the corner of her eye.

He stood over by the picture window near the front door. He'd pushed the curtains aside enough to peer outside. He scanned the front yard, head cocked, listening for trouble. The darker shades of his bruised, purple halo shifted and swirled.

His hair had dried and set with the waves of his braid. It hung long, the ends brushing his belt. He'd removed his plaid over-shirt and hung it on the edge of the bar. He'd pushed up the sleeves of his black turtleneck sweater, the corded muscle in his forearms reminding me of the superhuman strength he'd once had. His bare toes poked from the wide hems of his black jeans.

Sunday didn't take any notice of me, of course, because I wasn't a part of the waking world. But Miguel did.

He turned to look directly at me. "'Bout time," he said.

I raised a brow.

"I called a bit ago," he said. "You were hard to get to. Your man did you well enough to really knock you out."

"Crude," I said.

"Could've been cruder. Not that y'all made that much noise, but the magic going off in there—a body would have to be dead not to feel it. You've got something special. It's a shame, really."

I stared at him, disbelieving the nerve it took for anyone to say something like that, much less a stranger pretending to be a friend. I couldn't resist the urge to look down at my body, to make sure I was clothed—or that my dreaming self was, at any rate.

Shirt. Jeans. Same thing I'd pulled on this morning after Miguel had tried to kill me.

"Nothing lasts forever." He sighed. "That's not why I called, though."

"Wait," I said. "How did you—"

"Call?" he asked.

I nodded.

"We're connected, you and me. Since you entered my mind back at your apartment this morning. You were worried using your magic on me gave the Order a line on you, but it was never them you needed to worry about like that."

"Because the chameleons operate separately from the Order," I said.

"In the ways that matter, yeah."

"So," I said, "what are you planning to do with your line on me?"

"Not much," he said. "We have that truce going."

It didn't feel that way, with him tapping into my mind. For all that I'd fallen asleep as unguarded as I'd been in a damn long time, all that was over in an instant. I looked at him like the threat he was, my mind turning over every angle I could use against him and every angle he might use against me.

"Did the oldest Watcher tell you something about having angel blood in you?" he asked.

"He did." I hadn't passed that information on to anyone yet. There hadn't been time or privacy. God, I hadn't even told Red when we'd had time and privacy. It hadn't been foremost on my mind. Maybe it should've been.

Miguel shoved his hands in his back pockets. "He's a douchebag, that guy, but he's not wrong."

"You know him?" I asked.

"From before today, you mean? Our paths have crossed." Miguel's tone turned derisive. "He wants the Angel, and he's willing to do anything to get him. Only with Shadow, it's that he wants something from the Angel. He'll do anything the Angel asks if the Angel will give him what he wants."

"And what's that?" I asked.

"No idea," he said. "That's the one thing I haven't been able to figure."

"Convenient," I said.

"No, not really."

"And you want to use the Angel," I said. "According to Shadow, that's what you're after. Taking the Angel from me. Taking my place as the Angel's vessel."

Miguel shrugged.

"What do you want him for, exactly?" I asked.

"Why would you believe anything I told you?" he countered.

I glared at him.

"Sorry," he said. "It's cultural."

"What the hell does that mean?"

He took a slow breath, longer on the exhale than the inhale, slowing his heartbeat. The Order taught that technique early and often. When you had a bunch of frazzled, anxious, freaked-out kids and not enough places for that energy to go, calming tech was a necessary part of training.

"It means that if you thought the Order in general was full of gunners ready to eat you alive and take your place at the top of the food chain, the chameleons are worse."

"I know," I said. "Only the strong survive, and other Darwinian bullshit."

He shook his head. "Only the strong who have the most angel blood in them survive."

Now we'd arrived at the heart of the matter. "Tell me."

He took a step toward me. "The Watchers are descendants of fallen angels, right?"

I nodded.

"Most of us with magic are descended from the Watchers."

Most. "Shadow said it was all angels, not just the Watchers."

Miguel took another step toward me.

I looked at his feet, then at his face again, my message clear. *Not one more.*

"There have been…infusions…of angel blood as the millennia wore on," he said.

"Angels mating with humans, you mean?"

"I guess that's possible," he said. "More like joining souls with them, becoming a part of them. Then the angel's power enters their blood. Their DNA. And they have kids, and so on."

"Sounds far-fetched."

"It's all far-fetched, Night," he said. "So are we when you get right down to it."

"So what's your connection with the Angel of Death, really? You—the other chameleons—did the Order use his blood to create you?"

He whistled. The dark patches in his halo stopped their shifting and flowed toward his body, hugging the edges of his skin like metal shavings clinging to a magnet. In this case, the effect was protective, and seemed utterly unconscious.

I'd hit his magical heritage on the nose.

"And me?" I asked. "What's so special about me that I can hold him?"

"There are angels, and there are *angels*," Miguel said.

They all seemed the same to me, especially when we were talking about apocalypse-level angelhood. I'd known a bit about all of that before I'd come to the Order because of my upbringing. When your parents thought you were evil, you looked for anything and every-thing to prove them wrong.

Once I'd become part of the Order, I'd learned a little more. Angels and demons and fairies were real, film at eleven. We had to know the basics in order to deal with any of those classes of beings if we ran into them during a mission. There were a lot of levels of angels. If we were talking about the ones up there in the hierarchy above the Angel of Death, we were in territory I'd prefer not to even think about, much less encounter.

"The angels supposedly closest to God?" I asked.

Miguel nodded. "Which of the angels closest to God might have enough juice to imprison the Angel of Death?"

"No idea," I said.

"There's one at the right hand," he said. "And there used to be one at the left, before he was cast down into the pit."

"Michael. Or Lucifer."

"One of those," he said.

"Which?"

"I don't know. I can't tell—can't read that deep into your blood."

"I'm not that special," I said. But then I thought about the chain of people who'd had a hand in putting out the hit on me when I'd been a child. The Watchers. The Angel himself. Which I now knew also meant the chameleons. That was a lot of power arrayed against one little girl.

If Michael's blood ran in my veins, what did that mean? What I knew about him flashed through my mind. Fiery sword of protection. Leader of God's armies. Defeated Lucifer and cast him down. Did possessing Michael's blood make me like him?

If it was the other one, what did that mean? Lucifer had been the light bringer, giver of forbidden knowledge. He'd refused to elevate humans above all other creations, to love them as God demanded. For his rebellion, he'd been damned.

I'd been a devil. I'd been a protector. One made the other possible.

"I can see the wheels turning," Miguel said.

I narrowed my eyes. "Stay out of my head."

"I don't have to be in your head to see what's playing across your face. Just think about it. That's all I ask."

I didn't like the mirroring of his words with Red's. I wanted it to be a coincidence, but like Red, I didn't believe in them.

"What did you overhear between Red and me?" I asked.

"Nothing," he said. "It's like…echoes. When I sent my call through the line between my mind and yours, I caught an echo of what had been on your mind as you fell asleep."

I didn't know whether I believed that. "Like I said."

He held up his hands.

"Why are you telling me all of this?" I asked.

"I've been trying to decide something," he said. "The chameleons sent me on this mission to find a way into your mind, to figure you out, learn your plans. I'm three for three there. But that wasn't all they wanted me to do."

"Shadow was right on, then," I said.

"Not quite." Miguel took another slow breath. "The original plan was to take over as the Angel of Death's vessel. That's what I was created to do. That's what I was sent to do. But once I got here—once

I got a glimpse into you—I realized I can't do it. I can't take him in because I can't contain him the way you do. You've got the archangel blood and I don't. So, I revised the plan. I was gonna take you over instead."

I wanted to be pissed, but here he was telling me, giving up any advantage of surprise. I wanted to poke holes, too, but this plan made more sense than the one Shadow had floated. A finger of fear touched my heart at the prospect, at the odds of Miguel succeeding, at what it would be like to be trapped inside my body with Miguel and the Angel in the driver's seat.

"Now that I'm here, and I've got you right where I want you, I'm finding I don't want to twist the knife," Miguel said.

Right where he wanted me? With a line between his mind and mine, and him having drawn my dreaming self to him. Everyone else in the house either asleep or unaware, emotional and physical reserves down to zero. Now was the perfect time for him to execute his plan.

"You don't want to," I said. "And why's that?"

"You and Sunday," he said.

I raised both brows. "We tortured you."

"Sunday tortured me."

"With my go-ahead," I said.

His voice softened. "I understand why you did it."

"Is that right?"

"Faith," he said.

It wasn't a difficult guess. I folded my arms across my chest.

"I could be useful to you and Sunday," he said.

"You think we want you to be useful?"

He chuffed. After a moment, he bent forward, hands on his thighs. "I knew you when you were little. You knew me, too."

"That was a long time ago," I said. "Too long."

"Not what you're thinking. Not after we became part of the Order. Before."

I cocked my head. "Before then, I lived with my parents in hell. You weren't there."

"Not with your parents," he said. "I knew your *abuela*."

"How?" I asked. "I barely remember her."

"She was my *abuela*, too. She wasn't related to either of us by blood, but by magic. She was a beauty." He closed his eyes. I could practically see the memories he drew up around him, they were so thick for him. "Hair as dark as midnight, with fine silver hairs all through it like spider-spun silk reflecting the moonlight. She never put it up—always wore it long, sweeping down to her waist. Her eyes were kind. Nothing got by her. She liked trousers. Her favorite pair was stormy-sky gray. She wore short cowboy boots with little heels, black with colored flowers embroidered on them. She liked button-down shirts, especially—"

"Blue," I whispered. "Powder blue."

I hadn't recalled any of that until he said it. But as he'd spoken, I could not only see her, I could smell her rosewater perfume.

"Her name was Dream," he said.

Which wasn't a name at all. Like the Watcher Shadow's name, it was a title.

I stared at Miguel. "She was, what—forty?"

He nodded. "She looked about that old, but she felt a lot older. As old as Shadow. She was just like him, Night. Ancient. Powerful."

I wanted to believe that he remembered her, that he hadn't gleaned her from my mind. "Can you take an image from someone's mind if they don't remember it in the first place?"

"No," he said. "The goal is to know enough about a target to impersonate them. If it's deep cover we're after, to know them so completely that you can become them. Forgotten events are usually buried so deeply that they don't affect a person's self-awareness or other people's knowledge or opinions of them, even if they do hold a subtle sway over behavior. In other words, they're not worth spending the time to uncover."

"What else do you know about our grandmother?" I asked.

"The taste of the *posole verde* she liked to cook. The stargazer lilies she cut from the garden, and the bright green vase she put them in on the wide sill of her kitchen window. Otherwise, nothing normal. She kept a collection of jars in her pantry. Some of them looked like canned stuff—jam, veg, fruit, pickles. But some of those jars, they looked like they held stars inside of them. Others held rocks so old, I could feel the weight of centuries when I held them. And then there's this."

He rolled up his left sleeve to show me a half-moon mark just south of his elbow. It looked like a regular scar, maybe from a fall or a run-in as a child.

I raised a hand to the same spot on my left arm. I didn't need to uncover it. Miguel knew it was there. He'd shown me his as proof that he was telling the truth.

"She marked us for what's coming," he said.

"What do you mean?" I asked.

"I can't be sure even now, but I'm thinking she worked with the angels. The big ones. I'm thinking she searched out kids like us, checked us out, maybe weighed our hearts like that Egyptian god, Anubis. Lighter than a feather, ascend to Heaven. Heavier than a feather, find yourself devoured."

I raised a brow. "Let me guess who we are in that scenario."

He set his hands on his waist. "She didn't visit everyone in the Order, or among the chameleons. We might be the only ones, so far as I can tell. But I'm betting we're not the only ones out there."

Odds were, he was right.

"We have a part to play," he said. "Which means that where you're concerned, the Angel of Death is supposed to be right where he is, with you."

From the corner of my eye, I caught a glimpse of Sunday stirring where she sat. The beanbag filling whooshed as she shifted her weight. It was ridiculous. It was real.

This conversation with Miguel was real, too, even though one of us was dreaming. He'd wanted to talk to me privately, so he'd found the only way to do that.

"It's great that you told me all of this," I said. "It's not every day I get to hear stories about my childhood that aren't horror stories— even if I'm not sure exactly what side of the line *Abuela* Dream falls on. I get why you wanted to talk to just me and not the others. You're trying to convince me that you're a friend, or more like a cousin. Why, Miguel? What is it that you want?"

"I want a chance," he said. "I'm no use to the Order, and by telling you all this, I'm no use to the chameleons, which makes me a dead man walking. If I'm going out—or if I make it through to tomorrow—I want to do it as myself. You think you can give me that chance?"

I didn't know whether I could, or whether I wanted to. He might hold other memories from my past, other secrets that I needed to know. He might be a true friend, or he might betray me. I'd known him once upon a time, but that time was over.

Letting him in meant taking a chance, not just for myself, but for everyone.

"How can I trust you?" I asked.

"I swear by the mark," he said.

Just words about a scar I didn't remember getting. But all the fine hairs on my arms stood on end, and the short, fine hairs on my scalp, too. I had no idea what had happened in the space of a few seconds, but I couldn't ignore it. More than that, I felt incapable of ignoring it, as if that mark had a resonance outside of Miguel and me.

Swearing like that—it meant something.

I filled my words with as much force as I could muster. "If you break that promise—"

"You'll kill me," he said. "Maybe I'll let you. It feels that way, doesn't it?"

It did. "Dead man walking."

He nodded.

He'd have to earn whatever trust I gave him, and he'd have to earn it in spades. "We'll see."

"You won't be sorry," he said.

"No way to tell yet."

"I think I understand about your family," he said.

I blinked at him. Him saying that seemed out of the blue.

He flashed a wry grin. "Or maybe I don't understand them, but I want to."

Miguel the chameleon, I didn't trust as far as I could throw him. Miguel the person might have a fighting chance. He was trying to be a person. I understood that all too well.

I'd been gone from the Order for years, but I was still trying to figure out how not to be an operative after all that time. Maybe I hadn't been able to stay in one place long enough. I hadn't learned how to just be. Everything the Order had taught me remained in my muscle memory, in the automatic responses that my training had instilled. I didn't want to have to play an angle anymore, or wonder what angle someone else played against me. I didn't want to be that person anymore. I wanted to be something else.

I'd tried to do that, to become something I barely remembered how to be: a human being.

"It might take a while," I said.

"The voice of experience?"

I returned his wry smile.

He went still, listening.

A half-second later, I heard what he did. The roll of tires on wet pavement. The splash of footfalls. There were people outside in the middle of the night in front of our hideout.

The steps drew closer to the house, but the sound of them faded halfway between the street and the porch, as if they dared not come any closer.

I closed my eyes.

My dreaming self snapped back into my body violently, like a rubber band stretched close to the breaking point. I sat bolt upright, all the heat fleeing from my body. The chill in the air was more than winter seeping through wood and sheetrock. My skin turned to gooseflesh. A brick of ice seemed to take up all the space in my stomach.

The floor beneath me felt hard as the concrete beneath the carpet, the blanket like a lead weight. Beside me, Red twitched.

I reached to shake him, but he'd already opened his eyes.

One glance at me and he rolled to his feet. He grabbed his boxers and jeans, tossing mine over to me. "What happened?"

"Someone's outside," I said. "Chameleons. Order. Watchers. Don't know which."

He rolled of the blanket, grabbing for clothes, pulling them on. "How do you know that?"

"Miguel," I said.

"Did he hurt anyone?"

I dressed as quickly as I could. "No. It's not like that. We had a talk while I was dreaming."

We hurried to the front room, racing past the closed door of the kids' room. In the far corner, Ben and Jess stirred.

Sunday lay facedown in the center of the room. Incapacitated, but moving. Conscious. She'd covered her eyes with her hands.

Miguel hovered over her, sparks dropping from his fingertips and turning to ash before they landed on the rug.

"Night?" Sunday called, louder than I expected.

A feeling of *wrongness* washed over me. I looked at Miguel. "What happened?"

He took a step back from Sunday. "She heard the Watchers a second after you snapped back into your body. I tried to explain what we talked about and what was going on, but she didn't believe me. She thinks I'm in league with the Watchers."

"What you are is a fucking dead man," Sunday said. "Motherfucker used my own magic against me. How could he have done that? How?"

He'd blinded her. Holy shit.

"Let her go, Miguel," I said.

Sunday sucked in a breath. "That's all? Take him out, Night."

When Sunday used her magic, she was the only one who could undo her work. She had to unravel it herself. Or if she was killed, the magic would dissipate. That was how magic worked. A fundamental principle. If Miguel refused to release her, that left only one option.

Miguel's hands stopped sparking. He shook them out and moved toward the window, pushing the drapes aside to peer out. "It'll pass in a couple of minutes. We've got Watchers. Half a dozen."

Sunday gritted her teeth. "Is Shadow with them?"

"I can't see him," Miguel said. "Doesn't mean he's not there."

He was definitely there. And there would be more Watchers around back.

Sunday gasped. "I've got shapes now. Edges."

Thank God.

In the corner, Ben pushed to his feet and drew Jess up with him. "Night? What's going on?"

"Wake Faith and Corey," I said. "Now."

He scrambled to his feet and ran.

"Colors," Sunday said.

Miguel glanced at her.

A few seconds later, Sunday blinked. "I can see," she said. "Everything's just a little blurry."

That, too, would resolve. I looked at Miguel. "You attacked her because she didn't believe you."

"Self-defense," he said.

"We're on the same side now," I said. "You understand what that means? We don't use our magic on each other. We use it to help each other."

Red broke in. "You want people to be on the same page, Miguel, stop talking to people in their dreams and say what you mean out loud."

Ben, Faith, and Corey came to stand beside him. The girls didn't look like they'd had any sleep. They looked keyed up. Ready to fight.

Sunday let go of my hands, pushed up, and rolled back on her heels. She looked at me ruefully. "Please tell me that while you were—what'd Red say?—talking in your sleep, you two geniuses formed a plan?"

"*We* didn't," I said. "I did."

Actually, although the first inklings of it had begun during Miguel's and my conversation, the rest of it had come together in my head during the last few minutes.

All eyes turned to me.

"It depends on you, Miguel."

He stared at me.

"You can't be serious," Sunday said.

I combed my fingers through my hair. "It's a risk because we're gonna be playing mind games with a bunch of Watchers. Miguel, how did you use Sunday's magic against her?"

Sunday turned her baleful gaze on him.

"I've spent a little time with her over the last day and night," he said. "It was enough to begin assimilating who she is."

"And that includes my magic?" Sunday asked.

Miguel nodded. "It's the last piece. I can learn a target. I can shift my physicality to look like them. I can show all their mannerisms, all their quirks. And if the target has magic, I can copy that, too. If I haven't had enough time to really understand their magic—where it comes from, how it works—I can do something that looks and feels like it, but the effects don't last long."

"Damn," she said, still mad, but impressed, too.

I could see the wheels beginning to turn behind her eyes and in her halo. The edges of the fiery red that surrounded her burnished gold.

"Miguel, you've had a deep line into my mind during all that time," I said.

He cocked his head. "I think I see where you're going with this."

"Me, too," Red said. "And I've gotta ask, to what purpose?"

A soft knock sounded at the door.

Miguel checked through the window. "Addie. She looks—" He bit back whatever he'd been about to say. "She's a messenger," he said.

"Not a trap?" I asked.

He shook his head. "I'd stake my life on it."

And all of ours.

Whatever Shadow had sent Addie to tell us, either she or her words would serve as a diversion. If we opened the door, we took the bait. If we didn't, Addie couldn't help us.

Couldn't help us?

That thought had come unbidden, with a brush of wings inside my chest. The Angel again. What in the hell was he doing? I couldn't risk him escaping here and now. There hadn't been time to deal with him, and there wouldn't be. All I could do was hold onto him as best I could—and pray.

"Night?" Red furrowed his brow.

I looked at all him, at all of them. Their faces were like my own, surprised and wary. I started toward the door.

Ben hustled to beat me to it. "I've got it."

I shook my head. "No."

"The shields that are guarding us here—the ones the Watchers are strengthening to keep the neighbors' prying eyes and ears away? Those are mine. They're tied to the house as a whole, but also to the doors and the windows. They're the natural defenses of the house. They stay closed and locked, the house is safer, right?"

I nodded.

"When we open the door, we're creating a breach in the defenses. I should be right there to strengthen them."

"You shouldn't be anywhere near the enemy," I said.

"We're counting on each other," he said.

He was a kid. He was powerful. He had an iron will and he wasn't going to back down. Either I trusted him, or I didn't.

"You'll be right behind me," he said.

Yes, I would. "Got your back."

He turned the deadbolts and folded back the hinged lock. He pulled open the door.

CHAPTER 7

THE SILVER FRAMES of Addie's glasses glinted under the tiny colored light strings that hung over the door. Her hair had come loose from the bun she'd worn it in earlier. It fanned out from her head, stiff and coal-dark. She wore a pair of brown sheepskin house boots, waterlogged around the edges. She frowned, pressing her lips together as if by doing so, she could hold herself together.

Her gaze slid past Ben and met mine. I saw terror in it.

"You want to come in?" I asked.

"I can't," she said. "Can I see Jess?"

The wind roared, sending a gust into the house. A wave of rain fell, striking the ground like pellets rather than drops. Not rain, then, but ice. I could smell the snow behind it, the frost and hush to come.

Jess edged her way toward us from the corner of the living room. I stepped out of the path between her and her aunt. Ben did not. The shield wasn't the only thing he needed to protect.

"You all right?" Addie asked.

Jess nodded. "What did Shadow do to you?"

Addie waved away the concern. "I'm fine. I'm going to be fine. I needed to see you, girl. I need you to know that I love you. Do you hear me?"

Jess went so still and quiet, when she blinked I imagined I could hear the flutter of her eyelashes. "You sound like you're saying goodbye. Please tell me that's not what this is."

Addie didn't answer that question. "You stay with Night. Whatever Night tells you to do, you do it."

Jess swallowed hard. Her aunt could no more promise this wasn't goodbye than I could promise we'd be safe. Too much was beyond our control. Addie had lied about being fine, but she couldn't lie about the bigger picture.

The idea that Addie had trusted me with Jess's well-being back at her house and that she'd just doubled down on it—that was as much a statement as to how Addie thought things would go as anything. She wanted Jess with me, and not with the Watchers. With an enemy rather than with her own people.

Addie had been loyal to them her whole life. To go against them—to prevent them from training Jess into her full power—the Watchers must have become something Addie could no longer countenance. Or they'd always been that, and Addie has only just figured it out.

"I need to deliver a message to you from Shadow," Addie said. "That's why he sent me up here."

Jess's jaw dropped. "You're still working with him?"

"Not *with* him," Addie said. "I'm doing what I have to."

"You were going to make me go with him," Jess said.

Addie looked at Jess as if she were a hundred kinds of fool. "Listen to me, Jess. You're learning early and hard that your elders are people. I've always tried to do the right thing, even if I haven't always done everything right. Sometimes I trusted my own elders when I shouldn't have. I walked a fine line doing that, and if you have to walk a line like that, whatever you're doing, it's not right. You understand?"

Jess shook her head.

Addie opened her mouth again, but seemed to think better of whatever she'd been about to say. She squared her shoulders and turned to speak to me.

"You know what Shadow wants?"

"The Angel," I said.

"You know how they want to take him?" she asked.

If what Miguel said about how and why I could hold the Angel, then chances were that the Watchers had the same problem Miguel had—not enough juice, or the wrong kind of juice, to get the job done. If I had the blood of one of the two archangels he'd mentioned, who had the blood of the other? Shadow? One of his minions?

"Does Shadow have the power to take me over? To put me under a spell?"

"You've been talking to the chameleon," she said. "No, he can't do that. He'll tear you apart."

Of course it came down to that. Neither the Watchers nor the chameleons could get their hands on the Angel without destroying me, whether that meant subjugating my mind, magic, and will, or taking my life. I'd imprisoned the Angel in my mind as an act of survival. I'd known there would be consequences, just not what they'd turn out to be.

What Addie described sounded like a fine way to kill me—but also like something else, something specific to Watchers' magic. "Tear me apart?"

"At a cellular level. He's close enough in lineage to the ones who made us to do that, or to get close enough to it that there'd be nothing left of you, Night. You been wondering what the Watchers really are, haven't you? What we can do?"

"Yes," I said.

"The Nephilim—those angels who created us—they hold the fabric of the universe together. All the worlds. Every one. The most powerful of us have power close to that level. I've got plenty of juice, but next to Shadow?"

Next to his supernova, she was only a ray of light, but one who'd just given me invaluable information about who and what we faced.

She leaned in close. "I'm the bait. He'll threaten to kill me, and you should let him do it."

I shook my head.

"If you come out there for me," she said, "he'll use the distraction to get to Faith. If he has her, he can control you. You know it's true."

I did. Faith was my greatest vulnerability. She was always going to be Shadow's play.

"Promise me you'll take care of Jess," she said. "Promise me you'll keep her safe. Make sure she gets an education. Make sure she grows up like she should."

I didn't say any of the trite bullshit that came to mind, like *You'll do that yourself after we find a way out of this mess.* Addie didn't apologize for not trusting me. I wasn't sure she did even now, but I was the best and only option.

"You have my word," I said. "And although I can't speak for Red, I know he feels the same."

Addie nodded. "I have to go back now."

I closed the space between Addie and Jess as Addie stepped away. Ben closed and locked the door. The *thunk* of the bolts sliding home felt final.

Jess barreled toward us, intent on mowing us down and following her aunt out into the freezing rain. I caught her in my arms and held her tight while she shook. We remained still while everyone around us began to move—to get dressed, to gather what gear we'd managed to bring with us in our flight to this place and whatever else the kids had the foresight to pull together in case of emergency. Doors opened and shut. People spoke softly.

When Jess's trembling had calmed, she whispered in my ear. "You can't let her die."

"I don't intend to," I said.

She struggled in my grasp, pulling away to look at me. Her eyes were dry, heat and light taking the place of unshed tears. "How?"

"Working on it."

"Work faster," she said.

"Understood," I said.

She pressed the heels of her hands into the hollows below her eyes and sniffed. Then she let her hands fall. "What can I do?"

"Ask Sunday," I said. "If there's nothing else, we meet back here."

Jess moved toward the back of the house in search of Sunday, just as I asked, leaving me a minute to myself in front of the fireplace, where the flames cracked a length of cedar, sending up a breath of fragrant smoke. I braced my hands on the mantel and leaned into them, letting the heat of the fire melt into me.

I let my mind go blank, allowing the muscle memory of my training to come to the fore, to see the angles I wished I didn't have to look for, to turn over the problem until the others returned. The pieces of information Miguel, and now Addie, had shared seemed as if they belonged to different puzzles, but the operative in me began to make sense of how they fit together.

Red's grass- and earth-drenched presence drew close behind me. I felt him before he laid a hand on my shoulder.

"We're here," he said.

I turned to look out at the living room and saw that everyone had assembled, waiting. I hadn't heard them. I hadn't sensed them at all.

Red's eyes crinkled at the corners in a show of calm and certainty I didn't feel inside and had no idea how he'd managed to manifest.

Sunday and Miguel stood side by side, leaning back against the bar. They didn't look ready to kill each other, or even as if they might be biding their time until they got a chance at it. Ben had taken up position near the door, his gray halo in constant touch with the house shield. Jess stood beside him, the shaking of earlier not only over but every trace of fear and anticipation of grief banished. She'd found a brown leather belt in the house stash, one with a sheath and a bone-handled knife that fit in it.

Faith and Corey held up the far wall, where a few hours earlier they'd watched a movie. They held each other's hands tight enough to cut off circulation. If there was a touch more gold in Faith's eyes than ought to be there, I couldn't do anything about it right now. They'd piled a few items in front of them. A couple more knives, a baseball bat, plastic water bottles filled with liquid that fizzed in ways water did not.

There were also extra coats and shoes, brought for those of us who'd fled Addie's place without ours.

"You with us?" Red asked.

This was my family. My reason for trying so hard to become human.

"Never anywhere else," I said.

Sunday studied my face. "You have a plan. Does it still involve Miguel turning into you?"

"It does," I said. "But there's more."

I told them what Shadow had said about humans with magic being descended from angels, which they met with stunned silence. And then I told them what Miguel had said about me in particular, about the specific angel blood that ran through my veins and granted me the power necessary to trap and hold the Angel of Death.

Michael or Lucifer.

Sunday glanced at Miguel. "Any way to prove that?"

"It's the lore," he said.

"It's a myth, you mean."

He shrugged. "You got a better explanation?"

"No," she said. "It just seems far-fetched."

"Like the Angel of Death is far-fetched?" he asked.

"No comeback to that," she said.

I pulled up my sleeve and pointed to the half-moon mark, the part of my physical landscape that every single person in the room except Miguel had taken for granted. "Jess, do you know what this is?"

She walked over to take a closer look. "No. What is it?"

"You ever heard of a being like Shadow—a woman whose name is Dream?"

"I only know Shadow," Jess said.

"She looks about forty, but she feels like an *abuela*."

Jess shook her head. "Shadow is with us. With the Watchers. He's the only one of his kind—that I know of."

Red reached for my arm, running his fingertips along the length and curve of the mark.

"You see anything?" I asked.

"Nope," he said. "Doesn't mean nothing's there, though. I'm used to seeing the same patterns in people—people aren't all that different.

Sometimes you have to know what you're looking for before you can compass it."

"Exactly," I said.

I'd explain later if I could. The important point was that the Watchers had a hole in their knowledge. And we could use that to our advantage.

I hoped.

I met Red's gaze.

He searched my eyes. "I'm not gonna like this, am I?"

"No," I said. "You and the kids stay in the house unless there's a compelling reason not to."

"Really not liking it already," he said.

I flashed him a tight smile, then glanced at the kids. "You hear that? *Compelling.*"

In other words, they had my permission to burn it up or burn it down if the need arose. It was the only way I could balance keeping them safe with the fact of their power, smarts, and teamwork.

"Sunday," I said. "Need you with me."

"I'm on it," she said.

I lifted my chin in Miguel's direction. "You ready?"

"You want me to go out the front door while you take the back," he said. Not a question, but a statement of fact.

"You're gonna bear the brunt of what they throw," I said. "It'll be your job to stand as long as you can."

"It's not a job," he said. "It's an adventure."

He wasn't really joking; he meant every word.

He was about to get the chance to take on a bunch of Watchers while wearing my face and using my magic, with no idea how long he could keep his feet or whether he'd end up dead for the trouble. I wondered about what he'd told me before about who he wanted to be —and how much having the chance to be someone other than himself for even a minute had to do with the strange joy that lit his face.

Sunday wore a similar expression. She'd been made for this kind of stuff.

I couldn't pretend that something inside of me sang, too.

Fucking Order operatives.

Corey and Faith handed me a pair of chunky Mary Janes, the ones Corey had worn earlier.

"We're about the same size," Corey said.

We were, shoes and clothes. I accepted the shoes and a black fleece jacket with gratitude.

"Give us a minute?" I asked.

Corey took a step back and went to help someone else, leaving me with Faith.

Definitely more gold in her eyes than there should've been. Her skin seemed burnished with it as well. The Awakened, closer to the surface than I'd witnessed before.

"I don't want to stay inside," she said.

"I get that," I said. "I don't want you to use our magic unless you have no other choice."

She slid her hands into her back pockets. "You're afraid of what will happen. That the Awakened will take over."

"You're not?" I asked. "After what happened at the gym?"

"That man needed killing," she said.

I flinched. "Never thought I'd hear those words come out of your mouth."

"I have to see it that way," she said. "If I hadn't killed him, he'd have killed Red and me."

Absolutely true. "I'm not gonna tell you different."

"Then what?" she asked.

I took a breath before I answered. "It bothered you before."

"That was before, Night."

I hugged her hard because I wanted her to know I loved her, but also because I didn't want her to see the worry on my face. That she hugged me just as hard helped some.

When I pulled away, Sunday stepped between us. "Now or never."

Miguel waited behind her. He'd taken up his long hair and tied it in a knot at the nape of his neck. "It'll go easier if I can touch you."

I held up my hands. He pressed his palms to mine.

A shock surged through me, raising every hair on my body to

attention. For a heartbeat, it felt as if every cell in my body had been invaded and sampled, as if someone had opened the door to my soul and looked inside, taking my measure. All the air in my lungs rushed out, leaving me gasping. All the air in the room seemed to gather in one point—over the crown of Miguel's head. It took the shape of a tiny, black dot, with weight and mass so great it might've been a planet instead of a speck.

My mouth leached dry as a desert. My lungs ached. My head began to feel full, like a fallen grape about to burst underfoot.

Then the speck above Miguel's head exploded. Air rushed into my lungs so fast and strong, I staggered back, breaking the connection between us. He began to change.

The transformation began with his hands, where we'd touched, his fingers drawing shorter, his wrists more slender. One piece of him at a time turned into a piece of me. Proportions shifted wildly. One eye his and one mine; one leg his and then mine. It felt like one part magic, one part science I couldn't name, and one part art. Picasso. Or Frankenstein.

I blinked at Miguel, and in that fraction of a second, he became a mirror image of me entirely—one swallowed by now-oversized clothes and shoes. The last change was the most important: his purple bruise of a halo darkened to the color of a moonless, starless midnight sky, the color of the beginning and the end, of birth and death. From darkness we emerged; unto darkness we would return.

"Wow," I said.

He flushed. A peculiar reaction. His voice sounded exactly like mine. "You saw how it works?"

I nodded. And then I got it—no one other than chameleons themselves had been allowed to see what he'd shown me. He'd given me clues as to how his magic worked, and therefore a potential weapon against him.

It was an act of trust. A leap of faith.

I nodded again, this time in appreciation.

"You understand how my magic works?" I asked.

"It's projection," he said. "I mean, it's more than that. You have to read the dreams and memories of your targets first. I'm not gonna have time to do that."

"No," I said. "You won't. So choose an image and project the hell out of it—at all of them. Into every single one of their minds. Have it ready before you even open the door and step outside. Hit them hard. Don't give them a chance to breathe."

"Got it," he said.

I felt a nudge at my elbow. Corey, with the rest of the clothes she'd brought, this time for Miguel to wear. If he was going out there as me, he'd need to dress like me.

"Thanks," I said.

Corey nodded. "I just hope it works."

"Me, too," I said.

I rested a hand on Miguel's—my—shoulder. "Good luck."

His lips—my lips—curved. "Yeah. You, too."

I headed for the back of the house, Sunday dogging my heels, and Red behind her. Before we reached the back door, at the end of the hall beyond the familiar places, Sunday had drawn her knife, keeping her gun in reserve—stealth first. She'd been outfitted by Corey, like me. In her case, with a purple fleece hoodie. She'd have looked silly if it weren't for the impending violence in her eyes.

"We'll need to move fast and silent," she said. "I'll only use this if I have no other choice."

Which meant magic. And for me, my knife as a last resort.

I recalled the terrain from the quick check I'd done last night. Patio right outside the door. No lawn furniture. Trees to the left— good hiding in there. Wood fence way out back. Trash bins on the right. Chain-link fence on that side of the yard, with a chain-link gate. There was a side yard, not fenced.

I glanced over my shoulder at Red. "Watch for infiltration. If the Watchers can get around Miguel or Sunday and me to get in here, they will. They'll go after—"

He finished my sentence. "Faith."

"Yes."

"They may get more than they bargained for if they try that," he said.

Vaporized, like the Order operative at the gym. I was more worried about the consequences. I didn't believe Faith's ends-justify-the-means conversion, and I sure as hell didn't want to see what the effect of further killing with her magic would do. If the Awakened rose in her full and whole—where would that leave Faith?

"Let's not go there if we can help it," I said.

"I know you want more time. I know we need it."

"Whether we get it may not be up to us," I said.

He planted a kiss on my mouth. It tasted like a promise.

"Come back," he said.

I held his gaze. "Whatever it takes."

Shouts filled the air out front. Some Watchers taken by surprise, from the sound. Others, not.

Sunday swung open the back door and stepped into the night.

I followed, the darkness swallowing me whole. I breathed in the scent of snow, and the sap-and-astringent perfume of the pine trees to our left. The soles of my shoes slipped and slid on the ice-drenched back patio. I could just make out shadows and edges, including the outline of the wooden fence at the far end of the yard.

My eyes adjusted quickly, but not fast enough to dodge the blade thrown at me. Sunday shoved me sideways. The knife flipped end over end, the point sinking halfway to the hilt into the siding beside the door as Red slammed it shut.

I caught sight of the Watcher who'd thrown it. Small frame. Auburn hair. Halo like a nebula. I reached out with my magic, locking onto her mind before she had a chance to figure out what hit her. A memory of Shadow flashed behind her eyes. He'd been at her with her own knife.

Addie hadn't been the only Watcher to have second thoughts about what Shadow had demanded of them. This one had tried to resist, but Shadow had broken her.

If I felt a sliver of empathy for her, I couldn't indulge it. Fast and silent, we had to be. I dumped her into that terrible memory as if throwing her over the side of a ship into storm-tossed waves. She sank like a stone.

She wanted to scream. Shadow wouldn't let her use her voice. So she cried out on the inside, heart racing so fast it would burst any second—

I set the trap that held her and pulled the rest of my mind, and my magic, back into myself.

Sunday was already moving again. I quickened my pace to catch her, slip-sliding again as cement gave way to slick grass.

The next Watcher went down before I could get to her. He was short, stocky, bald, and in a instant, blind. He dropped a handgun in the grass and drew his hands to his face. He rubbed his eyes, mouth open to suck in air.

Sunday had stopped to set her magic. She didn't make a sound—not even so much as the sound of indrawn breath. So the Watcher didn't hear her, but he heard me.

Down came the hands, reaching for the weapon he'd dropped. I launched a right hook at the side of his head. It connected with a sickening thud. Down he went before he could shout a warning. Sunday followed my strike with her knife.

I hunkered beside the chain-link fence, checking for movement, searching for halos. Rhododendrons lined the side yard, planted in a line of flowerbeds close to the house. Flowering bushes weren't the only things planted there, however.

Sunday knelt beside me. "Anything?"

"One pressed against the side of the house between the bushes," I said. "There's a couple more that I glimpsed a second ago closer to the front yard, but they were running toward the front walk. They're out of sight now."

"Miguel," Sunday said.

"Still alive." It gave me hope—a dangerous emotion to feel at a time like this. "I've got point from here on out."

I reached for the hidden Watcher with my magic, seizing their mind and dropping them onto a lonely road that stretched on forever under the Milky Way, an image they'd seen in an art gallery. The road was made for walking. If they became trapped there, they'd walk forever. No food. No water. No stopping.

I vaulted the fence and took off at a run, brushing by their unseeing eyes, flying down the side yard until I broke the plane of the house. I rolled, rising up again on the balls of my feet.

The movement caught the eye of a single Watcher whose gaze had wandered from the full-on assault three others levied against Miguel.

The Watcher's blue hair rose on end, impossibly tall. No, not hair —peacock feathers. The Watcher lifted a hand that glowed with blue fire and aimed it at me, using their magical muscles like a slingshot to draw back the shot.

They never got the chance to launch it.

Sunday barreled around the corner, skidding low to the ground, her eyes tracking the Watcher. She met the Watcher's gaze. A moment later, the Watcher hit the ground, blinded. Too far away for me to throw a punch or a knife, and I dared not tie up my own magic. Not with the field in front of me still in play.

The grounded Watcher screamed. Every single person in the yard froze.

The Watchers surrounding Miguel backed away—all except the one who'd managed to get hands on him. That one held him in a headlock, pressure on his jugular. As I watched, Miguel's consciousness fled. His legs betrayed him. He went down in a heap.

He kept my form, so the magic he'd attacked the Watchers with still held, and for all intents and purposes, the Watchers viewed him as if he were me. They'd laid eyes on me as well now. They mumbled their confusion, trying to work out which was the real Night. Which Night contained the Angel of Death, and which was the imposter.

I couldn't see Addie. I couldn't make out Shadow either, but I knew they were out here somewhere. If I tied up my magic on the remaining Watchers, I left myself open to his attack. And it was coming, as sure as the pellets of ice that fell from the sky gave way to big, wet, fat snowflakes. As sure as the houses all around remained dark and quiet. As sure as the sound of a far away train's horn penetrated the shields with a haunting moan.

I trained my magic on the Watcher who stood behind Miguel's fallen form. They were close to the house. A threat to those inside. I couldn't see them clearly against the backdrop of the house, but a silhouette would do just fine.

I dropped them where they stood into a vision of the train whose horn had sounded, onto the tracks beneath the train's wheels and weight.

Sunday took one as well, and then a second. That left only Shadow, wherever he—

I didn't have to wonder any longer. I saw him clearly, with his supernova halo, step from the front door of the house. He'd brought no one with him, and no one followed.

Blood stained his white-blond hair, and his pupil-less cobalt eyes glowed with barely suppressed rage.

Either he'd killed everyone in the house, or something terrible had happened, something he hadn't expected.

Sunday dropped her knife and drew her gun and fired.

My own fear rose up like a wild animal.

CHAPTER 8

SHADOW LAUGHED. The sound reminded me of the kind of darkness that swallows everything it touches, muffles every noise, and pierces the heart like a thousand obsidian knives only to soak up the blood as if it had never flowed—as if there had never been life or love at all.

The bullet Sunday fired exploded before it reached him, a ball of fire that vanished in an instant, raining ash onto the snow below.

Shadow stepped over the prone bodies of the Watcher I'd just dropped and Miguel, whose chameleon impersonation of me still held. He paid no mind to the Watchers Sunday had dropped as they writhed on the ground or lay still in shock, without their sight.

He searched the yard with his cold cobalt eyes, his gaze flowing over the rose bushes and the walk and the fat snowflakes that settled on the grass. No other magical attacks on the way. No one out here but the three of us.

When he looked at me again, I could see that he knew Miguel was the imposter, and that I was the real deal.

"How?" I asked.

"I read it in your blood," he said.

That made no sense. I wasn't bleeding. He had no physical contact with my blood. The things he was talking about being able to read were DNA-deep—or deeper. "You can just look at me and see that?"

"It's part of the fabric of your being," he said. "Those things are mine to see."

Addie had said the Watchers had the power to tear apart a person's being—or presumably, to knit them back together. Shadow was talking about Watcher magic, and as the oldest Watcher, his power in that area would not have been dulled or divided by space or time.

"A chameleon can copy many things," he said, "but the power in your blood is not one of them. I don't need to read your mind in order to know your thoughts," he said. "That's your department. But you should work on your poker face. You're an amateur, Night. Dream should've chosen better than you."

The other advantage I thought we had—the idea that the Watchers had never seen a mark like the one Miguel and I bore, that they'd never heard of Dream, that the power of an archangel in my blood might enable me to fight Shadow and win—went up in smoke.

I had nothing now except my wits. That wouldn't be enough against someone like Shadow.

I managed to keep that off my face, because damned if I'd let him know the despair that touched my heart. If I was going down—if I had to die—I'd make him work for it.

"Nice job, by the way," he said. "I didn't think you had it in you anymore, taking out my Watchers as if they were targets of the Order. I thought you'd gone soft."

"They knew what they were getting into, coming here with you," I said.

"They were ready to give their lives for the cause."

And they would, because I had no intention of releasing them.

Sunday sidled up to me. I didn't like what that might mean. It was better to give Shadow two targets than one, unless she meant to step in front of whatever he threw at me. I didn't want that.

She set her hands on her hips. "And what's that?"

"What it's always about," he said.

She tossed her head. "Well, it ain't money."

Shadow strolled across the lawn toward us. "So it's got to be power."

If Shadow managed to free the Angel of Death—however he did it—he'd be in over his head. "The Angel won't submit to you. If you think you'll be able to make him do what you want, you're delusional."

He shook his head. "The Angel of Death isn't my end, Night. He's my means. All I need is for him to walk free, to do what he plans to do anyway."

"What's that get you?" I asked.

"The keys to Heaven." He took another step closer. "That's what it's always been about. Too bad Addie won't be going home with us when the time comes."

"Where is the old lady?" Sunday asked.

"Inside," Shadow said. "Dying."

I felt no surprise. Panic, yes. I had complicated feelings about Addie, but Jess—Jess loved her aunt. And I loved Jess.

Sunday lunged for Shadow. I grabbed hold of her wrist hard enough to leave bruises. Hard enough to wake her up to the idea that attacking Shadow would be the last mistake she ever made.

"You want to go inside, Sunday?" Shadow asked. "I'll give you leave to go, but you might not like what you find."

She spoke through clenched teeth. "I'm not leaving Night."

"Even if the people in the house need you?" he asked. "Even if someone precious will expire without your attention?"

That was an obvious trap. Well-baited. So very hard to resist.

Sunday yanked her wrist from my grasp. "He could be talking about Faith, Night."

Yes, he could. "I don't want you to go, Sunday, but if it's Faith?"

She turned to meet my gaze, fear for me and the others etched around her eyes.

I leaned into her. She leaned back.

"It's okay," I said. "Go."

She moved toward the house, walking past Shadow without another word or a glance. I watched her go, the crunch of her steps supernaturally loud in the hush all around us. Once she made the walk and turned toward the door, I refocused my attention on Shadow.

Now that I had no guard to give him trouble, he moved closer, drawing nearer until he stood inches away. "A Watcher might be not be able to rip apart the fabric of your being without harming the Angel," he said, "but then I'm no ordinary Watcher."

"You're the oldest," I said. "You're special. Whatever that means."

He reached out to touch my cheek. At my answering glare, he stayed his hand.

"There are those of us who've been around since the beginning," he said. "Elders. The Angel is one. I am another. We're reclusive, mostly. We keep our secrets to ourselves, waiting for the signal that it's time to rise again, time to walk again, time to make the world ours again. Once there were many of us; now there are few. But there are still enough of us to take the throne of creation."

"The throne of creation? Is that some sort of euphemism for God?" I asked.

He shook his head. "It's a higher power than God."

Well, shit.

"I'm sorry to have to do this," he said. "Truly, I am. I'm loath to destroy someone my sister Dream has made her own, even if they're not worthy of that honor."

Shadow reached into me with his Watcher's power, brushing off my attempts to stop him, overriding my magic as if it were nothing at all. He took hold of my power with his mind and turned it over, examining its facets and ultimately discarding it in a cobwebbed corner as if it were something he'd dragged inside on the bottom of his shoe. It was worthless to him. Harmless.

He moved to touch me again. He had ahold of me—my mind, my magic. I couldn't stop him. His fingertips caressed my skin—then passing through it, reaching through flesh and bone into my blood.

I understood the title he bore suddenly, like finding revelation in a lightning flash. He only appeared to be solid, made from human parts. He only appeared to have weight and mass, to be one being, whole and contained within a sheath of skin that marked his edges.

In reality, he was a collective of shapes and darkness, as if all of the shadows cast by the sun and the depths of the human heart had taken refuge together. Burned together. Suffered together. Plotted together, sharing knowledge and manipulating each other and those around the collective toward a single, solitary end.

The shadows within him fluttered like crow's wings made of blackened steel and talons honed to the sharpness of a god's blade. Everywhere they brushed against a part of me, they cut and sliced and ripped and rent. They tore me apart as a predator tears prey. They tore me apart as if I were slag. Worthless. Harmless. Nothing.

I had no sight, no hearing—no sense at all except dissolution. My edges were gone before I had a chance to miss them, my bones broken and crushed, my magic squandered all except for the darkened door of my mind behind which I'd locked the Angel of Death. The Angel's cage.

The cage held.

Shadow turned all of his might against it. All of his fierce hope and pent-up rage. He began to chip at the lock, each blow glancing off the fortified magic that refused to yield, but leaving its mark, too. Chinks in the armor.

Inside the cage's confines, the Angel did not seem glad of it.

He didn't want Shadow to free him. He didn't want out at all. He bent his will toward keeping the cage secure, holding the magic intact, saving himself from the oldest Watcher.

Saving himself.

The power I'd used to hold the door closed had disintegrated along with the rest of my magic. The angel's blood in my beating heart might be worth something, but was it worth enough to keep the lock on the door?

The only thing holding the door closed was the Angel of Death himself.

As my mind began to disintegrate around the cage, I could see only fleeting images. The faces of people I loved. The people I'd tried to become human for. The people I didn't want to leave.

The kids.

Sunday.

Red.

Faith.

When I could no longer see the images, only feeling remained. My heart, like the cage, endured. It still beat—if not in my physical body, then on some other plane. That shouldn't be possible.

Heart.

Beat.

Blood.

Angel blood.

The blood of a high angel ran in my veins. I didn't know which, and I didn't care. They would know me for their own if they saw me, Miguel had said. They would know.

Would they hear?

With all the strength left in my beating heart, I sent out a call. For a single, endless moment, it seemed as if someone had answered.

The blackened steel feathers and talons went suddenly still. The snowflakes hovered in midair, turning like tiny, crystalline wheels. The stillness and the space between them seemed to go on forever, as if the whole world had drawn a deep breath and held it.

My heart began to slow, the space between the beats stretching out to minutes, to days, toward forever.

But then the snow began to fall once more. Shadow hacked at the cage. I would die, every piece of me shattered and scattered to the winds as if I had never been. Shadow would break the cage. It was only a matter of time. He would get to the Angel.

Whatever he intended for the throne of creation, whatever the fuck that was, the Angel of Death meant one thing: the end of the world. Of all the worlds.

Shadow bent the lock. Any second now, it would break.

Inside, the Angel roared.

A single, solitary hope formed in the moment before what remained of me imploded. A single, traitorous thought.

What if I turned the power of my blood toward a new purpose?

What if I stopped trying to contain the Angel of Death? What if I helped him instead?

I had no idea how to do that. I saw two possibilities, and two possibilities only if I made that choice:

Die without knowing what would happen. Whether Shadow would succeed, and what that would mean. He didn't mean well for anyone but himself. The world might burn. If it did, he wouldn't care.

Live, knowing that if I empowered the Angel, I might lose the ability to contain him. I might become his servant. The events he set in motion would lead the world to burn. I might have a hand in that. I might have no choice.

I was a chosen one of an Elder named Dream. I had a part to play in what was coming—but not if I was dead and gone.

The Angel of Death was my enemy—and my responsibility. I didn't know what I could do, if I could do anything at all. But I couldn't do it if I was dead and gone.

The people I loved would be in danger, and I couldn't protect them if I was dead and gone.

I had no time to decide. There was only now, or never. If I had a chance, I had to take it. I did the only thing I knew how to do, the only thing I could do. I barely knew how to do it. I had so little experience, and so much fear.

I opened my heart. I offered the Angel the power in my blood.

That offer of power did what Shadow hadn't been able to. It cracked open the lock on the cage.

The Angel absorbed the power in my blood. It entered him as a thousand rays of light, the fire of the sun meeting the darkness and decay. The heat and flame scorched him wherever they touched. He howled in pain, but still, he drew in the power.

The pain became agony, doubling and trebling like the pressure wave before an avalanche until it crossed a threshold of no return, until the force of it became too much to bear. The door of the cage burst open.

The Angel exploded into a thousand shards of fire.

Each shard sliced through Shadow's razor feathers and talons, the fire in them incinerating every shadow, illuminating every nook and small space in which Shadow tried to hide, leaving him no way to stay, and nowhere to go.

Shadow disintegrated, all that remained of him so much smoke that faded into the snow-drenched night.

The explosion of fire began to turn back in on itself—pulling in all the pieces that belonged, and nothing that didn't. The parts of me that Shadow had broken. The bits that had flown away on the wind. The flesh and blood and bone, come back together in the shape of a woman—my shape.

The Angel began to knit them back together again.

That remaking, that reweaving, was a Watcher's magic. The Angel was no Watcher, but he had the kind of power Shadow had—the power of an Elder being—and the remnants of the archangel magic that I'd given him.

When he was finished, when I had eyes to open and see with and skin to sense the ice in the air and the feel of the wind, when I could smell the snow again and taste the night on the back of my tongue, I found myself whole and hale, on all fours in the grass, lungs heaving for breath.

I willed my fingers to move, my hands to claw back toward my body. I willed the big muscles in my legs and core to draw me up to standing. My knees threatened to give way for a second, but decided to hold.

The Angel came to rest within me, just inside the edges of my skin. Any second, I expected him to take control. To take me over.

He did not.

I didn't know what that meant, only that I'd deal with it later. I had to get into the house now. For Faith and for Red. For Addie, who might be dying.

Someone was. I could taste it in the air. I could feel it, as if I were standing on the edge of a cliff at great height, balance tipping, helpless to stop the fall.

I ran, tripping over my own feet, then nearly tripping over the bodies of the Watchers Sunday and I had downed. I leapt over Miguel as his lashes began to flutter—as he started to come to. I bounded up the steps and burst through the door into chaos.

Sunday paced the strip of living room near the door. Her face was a mask of pain and rage and worry. Her palms were burned black. She'd tried to get past a shield and failed. She took one look at me and her eyes went wide.

I didn't want to know why. I didn't have time.

The shield that had flummoxed Sunday bore no sign of Ben's gray magic. This one had been woven of golden threads, and it undulated as if it were a living thing. A sparking, electric living thing. I couldn't see through it. I couldn't see anyone else except the person who'd made the shield and stood at its center.

Faith.

Her pupils bloomed with gold. No brown remained.

She'd glued her gaze to Sunday, as if Sunday were a stranger, a dangerous interloper. Faith glanced at me as I entered. She didn't seem to recognize me either.

I bit back the scream that wanted to roar from my throat. I kept my words even, and without any edge of magic. I didn't know the Awakened. I didn't know whether it had taken over utterly, or how much of Faith might still be in there.

"Let me in," I said. My voice sounded like mine, but not only mine. The Angel of Death's words twined with mine, adding power, adding demand, threatening force if necessary.

It was enough to shake Faith—or to shake the Awakened.

The golden shield faltered long enough for me to push through it, heedless of the threads that seared my skin and scorched my hair. Sunday had my back. We barreled into a circle of grief.

Ben knelt on a patch of blood-soaked carpet, cradling Addie's head against his thighs. Corey and Red had pulled every towel from the kitchen and bath to soak up the blood that seeped from the wound over Addie's heart. They applied pressure, while Jess used what magic, skill, and training she had to knit her aunt back together.

Addie's breath hitched. Her lips were pale, the color leached from her face.

Jess wasn't yet a full-grown Watcher. Her power had not yet filled out. She was losing the battle. There was too much blood and not enough magic to get the job done.

Red slid out of my way as I knelt beside Jess. He waved the others back. None of them moved an inch. Red saw me—and the Angel free within me. He gazed into my eyes with a trust that was total.

That trust settled into me, a cord of strength.

I focused on Jess. "I can lend you what power I have."

She looked at me, eyes going wide as Sunday's had done. "Please," she said.

I laid my hands on her back, magic flowing through my palms and into her, filling her with not only the power she needed, but the detailed knowledge of how to use it. How to weave a wound back together. How to set the healing. How to firmly reattach a soul on the edge of flight.

Addie didn't wake as we finished. Her deep color returned. Her breath evened to the deep, steady rhythm of sleep.

Thank God, or the throne of creation. Thank the Angel.

"She'll be like this for a while," I said. "One night, maybe two."

Jess let out a shaky breath she'd been holding. She reached for Ben's hand. Behind me, Corey scrambled to her feet and ran for Faith. I turned to look at my daughter—or the Awakened, a spike of fear piercing my heart.

But my girl's brow was furrowed, the corners of her mouth turned down, her eyes full of confusion. Her brown eyes.

Corey threw her arms around Faith, and Faith hugged her back just as hard.

I sat back on my haunches, rubbing my eyes with the heels of my hands. Red placed a palm in the center of my back, offering strength. Offering to take whatever I could lay onto him. Offering love.

I wanted what he had to give. I wanted nothing more than to be able to turn around and look at the man. But there was something happening inside of me, something that shook me to the core.

The Angel of Death surrendered the tattered remains of the magic I'd loaned him, letting it fall to pool in my heart once more. He walked back through the corridors of my mind into the cage I'd once forced him into, and drew the door closed behind him until it nicked shut. There was no bolt to be thrown, no lock to turn. There was only the Angel's inexplicable willingness to stay.

I cleared my throat. My voice was my own. Only my own.

"I need some air," I said.

Red rose behind me and hauled me to my feet. "Sunday?"

"I'll stay," she said.

I made my way out of the house, tottering a little underneath the Christmas lights that hung above the front door. The snow fell in a torrent, wind gusting. The whole world shimmered.

Miguel had pulled himself toward the porch steps and perched on the lowest one, head in his hands. He'd let go of my reflection, my essence—whatever he would call it. He was himself again, in too-small clothes so tight, they cut off his circulation. Snowflakes stuck to his hair.

"Did we win?" he asked.

"I don't know," I said. "We're all still here. Barely."

He gave us a thumbs-up. "I'm calling that a win."

I glanced past him at the fallen Watchers, the ones trapped in their own nightmares and the blind ones, all of them on their way to frostbite. What the hell were we going to do with that many incapacitated, magical freaks? The shields would have to come down eventually, and the sun would come up. And I didn't think Sunday had packed any extra zip ties.

A flash of light in the near distance caught my attention. I didn't believe my eyes at first, so I blinked, but when I looked again, nothing had changed.

Someone—or something—stood across the street. His hair was made of fire, writhing flames of orange, yellow, red, and blue. He had three eyes, two where I expected them to be and one in the center of his forehead. He wore golden armor that glittered like diamonds, and a sword with a golden hilt sheathed on his back.

He stood on the snow-dusted grass in front of us as if he'd come to view a curiosity.

A second later, he ceased to look all that interesting, at least on the surface. He was just a regular guy, if a regular guy could emanate enough power to bend the air around his body. He wore a pair of faded jeans and a black T-shirt with the name of some heavy metal band I should remember but for the life of me couldn't. He had black hair, short and thick, and eyes the color of the sun.

I became afraid to blink, wondering whether something had broken in my brain and I'd started to see things, worrying that if I closed my eyes even for a second, my imaginary man with fiery eyes would vanish. But then he disappeared anyway, winking into nothing as I watched.

Miguel whistled. "Anyone else see that?"

"What the hell was it?" Red asked.

"Archangel," Miguel said.

I'd called one. He'd finally decided to show. "Michael."

Miguel glanced over his shoulder at me. "Michael."

Fiery sword of protection. Showed up to take a gander, but not when I'd actually needed him.

"Asshole," I said.

Miguel raised a brow.

"He's late." I turned on my heel, straight into Red.

He wrapped his arms around my waist and started to say something, but whatever he'd been about to utter faded. He looked past me, finally managing a word. "Jesus."

The downed Watchers were gone. Poof. Vanished. No more muss, no more fuss. No more enemy at the gates.

"I guess we won't have to worry about how to clean all that up," Red said. "Think they're gone for good? Or should we expect them again sometime soon?"

"They were Shadow's people. Shadow's gone," I said. "And now so are they."

"I think the asshole gets points for that," Miguel said.

I laughed, mostly because if I didn't find the humor, I might cry. I could cry all night, in fact. "That's because you're grading on a curve," I said. "Let's go inside."

CHAPTER 9

I T TOOK A WEEK for the sound and fury to die down, for the foot of snow that had fallen to melt, and for some semblance of normalcy to return. Wounds healed. Bloody carpets were cleaned. I got used to the idea that I'd been torn apart and knitted back together by an archangel whose blood ran in my veins. Just another day in the neighborhood.

I woke on a Tuesday morning and drove my Honda down to the gym, as if it were any normal hour before dawn. I stood under the awning and turned my key in the lock. The December chill sliced through my black fleece hoodie. The mist in the air coated my hair and snuck in through the open spaces at the neck, sending a shiver all the way down to the soles of my feet.

The traffic light at the corner to my left flipped from red to green, the hum of engines and the slick of tires on wet concrete a comfort to my still-exhausted nerves. I paused a moment, listening for anything out of the ordinary. Nothing stood out other than the most dependable sound in the world.

Down the way to my right, materializing from between the rows of parallel-parked cars on either side of the street, the man I'd dubbed the Orange Warrior rode by in his neon-orange rain suit, bike tires splashing through the puddled light of the street lamps. He flashed the peace sign, just like he did every morning.

"Hey! Night!"

"Morning, Charlie!" I called, and gave him the usual thumbs-up to carry with him on his way to work. His golden halo flashed as he sped around the corner.

Footfalls sounded behind me. Red, carrying a tray filled with the largest coffees the diner across the street offered, along with two bagel sandwiches wrapped in parchment paper.

"Extra bacon?" I asked.

"Questioning my integrity this early in the day?" He rolled his eyes. "A promise is a promise, Night."

I flashed a half grin and pushed open the door for him. I got the lights, too, turned off the alarm, and followed him down the steps to his office.

He shared out the breakfast and sat heavily on one of the two blue and silver visitor chairs on the near side of the desk, pushing the other out with one foot as an invitation for me to settle beside him. His hair was still wet from the shower, the ends curling from the humidity outside. He'd shrugged on a dark green down jacket over his hoodie as an extra layer against the cold.

He took a sip of coffee, watching me lower myself slowly into the seat.

"Still hurting?" he asked.

I frowned. "I guess I'm not hiding it that well."

"No need to," he said.

"I don't like to be that person."

He raised both brows. "The one who needs help and has to ask for it?"

I toasted him with my cup of joe. "That's the one."

"It's okay," he said.

I set down my cup, sliding it back and forth on the desktop. "It's the kind of thing that would get you dead in the Order—admitting weakness."

"That's inhuman, Night. You know that, don't you?"

"Yeah, I do." I met his gaze.

He searched mine. "How's the Angel of Death? Still playing hermit?"

I nodded. "I don't know why he hasn't broken free. And before you pose the question, yeah, I've tried talking to him. He doesn't answer. It's disconcerting."

"There's a whole lot about it that's disconcerting." Red brushed his hair back from his forehead.

"The lock on the door is reconstituting itself, I guess because my blood is doing the same as I recover. It may take a while to fully reform, and I don't know whether it will ever be the same again."

I might take a while, too. Whether I'd be the same again, I had no way to know.

"You're worried," he said.

I shook my head. "I'm afraid."

He grinned. "How hard was that to say?"

I deadpanned. "You have no idea."

His smile faded. "What are you thinking?"

Thoughts that no one should ever think. "I need to hunt down an archangel."

He mulled that over. "You think you'll get answers that way?"

"Maybe not," I said. "But it's a place to start."

There was one other place I could go for information, but the odds were high that I'd die in the attempt. "The Order will have archives to rifle through."

"Or archivists to torture," he said. "Sunday could probably get down with that."

"Not funny."

"No," he said. "It's not. What about the Watchers? With Shadow destroyed, they might be in a place to renegotiate their aims."

I bit my lip. "You know, I get the feeling that Shadow's not dead."

"The feeling?"

I nodded. "It's visceral."

"In your gut?" he asked. "Or in your blood?"

"Good question." More mysteries to unravel.

"Lots of questions," he said. "Including what's going on with Faith and what we're gonna do about that."

Of all the things I feared, losing Faith was the worst. She was holding it together for now, and her friends were helping her. But they couldn't stop the god inside of her from waking completely, or handle what might happen on their own.

The bunch of them had stuck to our pact not to keep secrets. They were looking for another hideout in case we needed one. They kept me in the loop. Still, choices had consequences, and my choosing to help the Angel of Death was a problem for them—even we were all alive and whole because of it. I could see it in the speculative glances Jess shot my way, and the way Corey listened too carefully when I spoke, as if she still heard the Angel's voice woven with mine.

Every single one of them understood that I'd die before I allowed the Angel to harm them. That made all the difference.

I didn't yet know what to do about the Angel, and I'd have to live with that until I figured it out.

There was one thing I couldn't live with any longer, and I'd suggested Red come in with me this morning because I wanted to talk with him away from prying ears and prying eyes. Corey had stayed over last night, talking and giggling with Faith until the wee hours.

"So, we're back to needing answers." I said.

Red leaned back in his chair. "Why do I get the feeling we're changing the subject?"

"Because we are," I said. "I am."

"What do you want to know?"

I took a deep breath. "All the things we talked about that night, before the violence?"

He nodded. "I meant every word I said."

I held up a hand. "I know."

He tensed. "But?"

"No but. It's not like that."

I turned over in my head all the ways I'd avoided saying what I felt, the reasons and the excuses. I'd avoided it because admitting vulnerability would make me less than the perfect machine I'd been trained to be. I'd been afraid of not being enough. Of not being human, able to let go of what I'd been so that I could become someone new. Keeping my feelings close to the vest had felt safe. Secure. And lonely as hell.

Maybe it was all right if what had happened that night changed me permanently. Maybe it was all right if I was never the same.

I was no stranger to chance, clearly. I'd taken every one I'd needed to when the stakes were impossible. Every single one, except the most personal, the one closest to my heart.

I took another breath, not because change that scared me, but because after everything that had happened, I refused to let fear stop me.

"Night? You want to ease up on the suspense?" He studied my face.

I met his gaze and held it, choosing my words with care. "This is about the thing you didn't say."

He put his cup down, his hand shaking a little.

"Maybe you didn't want to say it then," I said. "I can think of a lot of reasons why that would be. But I'd rather not guess, and I'd rather not play anymore, so I'll say it now."

He waited, holding his breath.

"I love you," I said.

I accepted all the vulnerability that came with loving him. I let that show on my face. I needed him to know. I needed him to understand.

For a long minute, I thought he might stare a hole straight through me. But then his face lit from the inside, his halo glowing as bright as if the sun shone inside of him, and all of my worries fell away.

He leaned forward in his seat. I met him halfway. I memorized the feel of his lips on mine, the taste of him. I shivered as he whispered to me, because of the tenderness in his voice and the feel of his breath on my skin.

"I love you, too," he said.

A heartbeat later, a knock sounded on the door.

I blinked at Red. "No one else should be here this early. Miguel's not coming by for like half an hour."

"No one ever knocks," Red said.

We got up together and headed for the door. Once we reached the top of the stairs and I caught a glimpse through the glass of the visitor's tiger-striped halo, I pushed Red behind me.

"What is it?" he asked.

Our visitor didn't mean to kill us, or we wouldn't have known what hit us. That didn't mean I had no reason to worry. "No one good. Stay here."

He set his jaw. "The hell you say."

I spoke with all the force I could muster. "Then stay behind me."

By his silence, he acquiesced to that much.

I marched toward the door and pulled it open. Outside, the mist had given way to rain, and the woman at the door had seen her share of it already.

Her auburn waves were plastered to her head, drowned-rat style. She wore black from head to toe, chic and practical, except for the lack of a hood on her coat. Her hazel eyes took in every detail of my appearance, and of the menace in Red's posture and expression behind me.

Menace was a one-hundred-percent appropriate reaction to this woman, although the first time I'd seen her, I'd thought she was my savior. I'd been a child, and she'd pulled me from the hell of my life into a fancy car with fancy words, promising me a place to belong. A place where I'd never have to deny my magic or worry that using it was wrong.

She'd saved my life, and she'd ruined me forever.

Her halo undulated as if muscle moved beneath its surface. She was a predator, no mistake.

"Mentor," I said. "I'd have heard about it if you'd left the Order, and I haven't heard a thing."

She shook her head, once. "I'm here on Order business, Night."

"What business is that?" I asked. "Picking up some miserable, magical child to bring them into the fold? Infiltration? Murder?"

"We have a sticky situation," she said. "One that we need your help with. Come find me when you're ready. You'll know how."

The fact that she'd come here at all set off every alarm under my skin. The fact that she'd asked for my help—the Order of the Blood

Moon had asked for my help—marked a sea change I didn't know how to measure.

These people had spent years hunting me down, trying to kill Faith and me. They'd sent operative after operative, and I'd sent them all back in a body bag.

We were never going to be friends. I never wanted to be allies. What the hell had happened to bring her to my door?

I said nothing to my mentor. She knew my thoughts perfectly well. She'd raised me, after all.

"See you later," she said.

I stared after her as she turned on her heel and walked back into the rain, cutting through the darkness until she became one with it, her steps silent as the grave.

If you enjoyed this book, please consider leaving a review. It doesn't have to be long—even a few words will be very appreciated.

Reviews make it possible for an author to continue writing books in a series. They make a big difference in helping to get the word out about a book or a series. And reviews can make the all difference in the world when a reader wants to take a chance on a new author, but isn't sure whether they will like the book.

Thank you for taking hours out of your busy life to read. I hope this book brought you time to escape into a story, and that it brought you joy.

Turn the page to read Chapter 1 of **Angel Falls**, Book 3 of the *Soul Forge* series.

ANGEL FALLS - CHAPTER 1

I CLOSED THE FRONT DOOR of Justice Gym, peering through the glass into the darkness before dawn. A scan of the sidewalk and the street on the other side showed nothing except an early Monday morning drenched in December mist. Tires slicked on wet pavement and engines hummed. Normals on their way to work grabbed breakfast and coffee at Stumptown Diner across the way as if nothing earth-shattering had just happened.

As if the dangerous, powerful woman who'd been my mentor in the Order of the Blood Moon hadn't just shown up out of the blue, asked for my help, and then vanished.

That she'd found me didn't surprise—I'd made a stand in Portland. No more running. Nowhere to hide. That someone who'd spent so much time hunting me and mine with the intention of killing us would ask for my help?

Under my black fleece hoodie, my skin turned to gooseflesh. The soft fall of the mist took on a sinister sound, the morning's peace irrevocably shattered.

I performed a second scan of the street, this time with my magical vision. I shifted my sight, studying the halos of the people on the street, the fields of life force that surrounded every living person. I searched for everything from ill intent to unnatural attention.

Nothing.

There was only the world outside, and the gym inside, with its perfume of rubber and sweat. The elevated waiting area with its brown suede, people-eating sofa crouched on my left. The empty black cubbies against the wall. The short open staircase that led down to the office and workout space.

Not five minutes ago, I'd risked my heart in a way I never had before. I'd told Red Jennings that I loved him. He returned that love in spades. In spite of the chaos all around us, we'd found something precious.

He stood behind me now. He had my back, and I had his.

"She's gone for now," I said. "Along with her backup."

Red's faint Texas drawl grew more pronounced with each word. "I didn't see any backup. Just her."

"Standard operating procedure when walking into the den of the enemy," I said. "There was backup with her, and they left with her."

"That's why you only listened," he said. "You didn't throw down."

I nodded, then glanced over my shoulder to meet Red's gaze. I read worry in the lines around his green eyes, but not a single trace of fear.

His shaggy salt-and-pepper hair was still wet from the shower, the ends curled. He still wore his dark green down jacket against the cold. We hadn't been inside long enough for him to take it off.

"Tell me about her," he said.

"Her name is Lily." I moved past him, descending the steps two at a time onto the gym floor. I made a beeline for the garage doors at the back.

Red dogged my heels.

"She was my Mentor inside the Order," I said. "She recruited me. She picked me up on the street outside my house the night after it burned down and brought me into the fold."

Red had been my next-door neighbor at the time. He'd been sixteen. I'd been twelve. He'd saved my life, and then I'd disappeared into the arms of the Order.

The Order gathered every child with magical ability its recruiters could find. It trained them to use their magic to kill. The Order's objective had always been a mystery, even to its operatives. I hadn't cared. I'd only wanted revenge on the people who'd hurt me and those like them.

It wasn't just that, though. I'd been devoted to the Order because it was the only place I belonged. I'd been a good killer. I'd enjoyed it. The world was a bad place, and the people I'd targeted deserved what they got. I'd believed that with every fiber of my being, once upon a time.

I jogged across the gym floor past barbells, plates, racks and pull-up bars, interlocked black rubber mats on the floor dulling the thud of my step. The garage doors were still locked. A small window beside them provided the only view out. I scanned the rough asphalt parking lot out back and the high weeds that lined the chain-link fence on either side. No sign of foul play or anyone watching. The street looked clear, too. Just parked cars slumbering along the curve of the far curb and the glow of Christmas lights hung on the eaves of the houses and four-plexes.

There was no other way in or out of the gym. Not perfect, but decent for defense. Two exits were better than one if we were forced to leave.

Red caught up, slowing to a stop beside me. "Lily's like you?"

Lily had done her best to turn me into a reflection of herself. Deadly. Heartless. It hadn't turned out the way she'd planned.

"No," I said. "Mentors like Lily are predators. They're also a kind of judge, jury, and executioner. Potential operatives don't make the cut? The mentors do the culling."

I heard myself say those words as if I was talking about opening the fridge to retrieve a late-night snack. It was cold, but that was how things were. Colder still? The murders I'd committed under orders, what taking those lives had done to my victims' people, and what the killing had done to me.

It had shattered my soul.

In the end, I'd left the Order. Therefore, I could not be allowed to live. The Order hunted me mercilessly. Sent operative after operative after me, and then finally the Angel of Death. Yet Lily had made no magical attack at the door. She'd brandished no physical weapons. She hadn't even threatened.

She'd asked for my goddamn help.

She hadn't said what for, only told me to find her when I decided one way or the other. As if I had a choice. And then she'd just walked away as if we weren't mortal enemies.

"So this is it," Red said. "When you made the decision to stick here and not to run anymore, you declared war against the Order. And now they're coming to the fight."

"I wouldn't have put it exactly that way," I said.

Lily had knocked politely and asked her question. I couldn't believe a single thing about her—nothing she said, nothing she did. There would always be an ulterior motive. Not all wars were hot, with magic flung and bullets flying.

"But I'm right," he said.

I nodded.

"I'm out of my depth with these people," he said.

His magic was solid, but not offensive in nature. He saw through to the heart of a person—what made them tick, what was real. He could recognize the good in someone even when they couldn't see it in themselves.

He owned this gym. He had regular customers, but in and among them, he had taken in magical kids, including mine. He'd given them somewhere to go to keep out of trouble. Someplace they felt at home.

He'd taken me in, too. Given me a home. Given me his heart.

"The kids will be here any minute," I said.

"You sure that's a good idea, them being here?" he asked.

"No," I said. "But it's too late to head them off."

He reached for my hand, twining his fingers with mine. "I'm here."

I squeezed his hand. "I know."

It meant the world to me that he'd gone all in on being with me. He'd grown up in a very different world than I had, with his share of hardships to be sure, but not with violence and obedience and brainwashed belief. He'd had a quiet life before I'd walked back into it. Neither of us wanted to lose each other again.

The fact that he stayed, that he committed to taking on my trouble—I knew what it meant to him. I also knew what it could cost him.

"We need to go on lockdown," I said. "Everyone accounted for, where we can keep them safe."

The gym had some magical protection that Red had laid down and that I'd augmented, but not enough. I could ask the kids to leave here and head out of town, but I knew they wouldn't go. They'd proved that by now.

We had a local Watcher—a descendant of fallen angels—on our side. Her house was our best bet.

"Call Addie and let her know what's up," I said.

Red pulled out his phone without a word.

I did the same, dialing my closest friend: Sunday Sloan, who had been my only friend inside the Order, and more than that for many years. She'd followed in my footsteps, leaving the Order to fight by my side after the Angel of Death had come to town. She'd risked her life, and she'd killed, and in the end I'd defeated the Angel in a battle of mind and will. I'd imprisoned him in my mind.

Sunday could've moved on then. Instead, she'd stayed. I trusted her with my life. I trusted her with my everything.

She was not a morning person. She picked up on the fifth ring.

Even jolted from sleep, her voice was musical, like the sound of water flowing over rocks. "Who died?"

"Lily was here," I said. "She wants my help."

I heard the creak of bedsprings and then a sudden echo as Sunday put me on speaker. "The hell?"

"I need you and Miguel," I said. "Can you meet us at the gym?"

She hesitated, leaving me with the slide of drawers opening as she dressed.

Miguel was our newest team member, if our group of former assassins, gym owners, and high school kids could be called a team. Sunday and I had known him when Lily first recruited the three of us into the Order. During a harrowing river survival test, he'd vanished.

We thought he'd drowned, but it turned out he'd been pulled into a shadow organization within the Order that tended the Angel of Death —the chameleons.

Unlike other magical beings, chameleons weren't born. They were created.

Miguel's innate magic had been altered. He'd been remade into one of them. He could look like anyone he wanted to. He could assume another person's magic as well.

He'd been sent to jailbreak the Angel from the prison of my mind. Instead, he'd ended up on our side, and put his life on the line. Even that wasn't enough for Sunday to trust him.

I had only slightly more faith in him than Sunday did—ten percent trust and ninety percent wait-and-see. But it was go time, and he had our Order training plus a damn fine, creepy-as-hell chameleon skill set that we might need.

"Ten minutes." She hung up.

A knock sounded on the front door. That would be the kids.

The jingle of keys confirmed my guess. The door opened, the electronic chime echoing against the concrete walls.

My daughter's voice rang out. "Night? Red?"

I raised my voice to carry. "In the back. Lock the door behind you."

Red and I made our way toward her, and met her at the bottom of the steps while the others who'd come in with her dumped their stuff into the cubbies upstairs.

Faith's brown eyes were still sleepy and threaded with gold. Her silver halo was streaked with gold as well. I could make out the impression of a pillowcase wrinkle on her right cheek. Her long black hair fell in waves to her shoulders. She wore a purple T-shirt under her hooded black coat, along with black leggings and black sneaks. She held her black backpack by one strap, dropping it on the floor with a thud at the sight of my face. She blanched, her light brown skin turning a shade paler.

Then she held still for a moment while Red took a good look at her, making sure that she was who she appeared to be. We'd had "visits" from chameleons other than Miguel. Checking each other like this had now become part of our normal protection protocol.

Red gave her the thumbs-up.

"What happened?" she asked.

"The Order," I said.

"Here to kill us?"

"Eventually," I said.

She cocked her head. "But not right now?"

"No," I said.

She rolled her eyes. "They shouldn't keep trying. It's embarrassing."

I stared at her.

"What?" she said. "It's true."

"Maybe so," I said. "But once upon a time the Order scared the crap out of you. And they should."

"That was before, Night."

Before, in her former life, back when we'd been on the run. Before the Angel. And before we'd discovered that in addition to having the power to talk with gods, Faith carried a god inside of her.

That god was called the Awakened. A misnomer, because the Awakened had slept for thousands of years, its soul—or whatever spirit gods possessed—passing from one magical human to another across time.

According to our Watcher, Addie, the Awakened was a big deal, even if no one knew exactly what it was. The thing we did know: the Awakened had begun to come alive within Faith. The gold in her eyes was new, and belonged to the god.

The Awakened had saved her and Red's lives when the last Order operative to come after us had tried to take them out. It had saved them by vaporizing the operative.

I'd been waiting for Faith to break down over having killed a man, even if that man had tried to kill her. She still carried an innocence inside of her, and a tender heart. But she'd held it together. I didn't know how.

The Order had brought us together. She'd been my last mission—

she and her family. I'd ended her parents, but I hadn't been able to kill a child, so I'd taken her and run. That was why and how I'd left the Order, and why and how she'd become my family.

Hearing her talk about how Order operatives should feel embarrassed by their failures might be appropriate on one level, but it didn't sound like her.

Red cleared his throat. "I need everyone down here now."

The other three kids made their way down the steps, decked out in their gym clothes and, like Faith, a little bleary-eyed. Red scanned them as they descended.

Ben served as the unspoken leader of the group. His long, brown hair and even longer bangs hid half of his face. He had a thin nose, a meticulously groomed soul patch, and a halo that might as well have been a gray stone wall.

Ben was a shield. No magic could penetrate the barrier of his halo. He could shield himself and at least one other person if they stuck close.

Jess was Addie's niece, and Watcher-in-training herself. Her halo looked like a night full of stars. She'd twisted her dark, kinky curls into a loose bun on top of her head. Her favorite gold hoops dangled from her ears. She was all of five feet tall. Easy to underestimate, but she was strong, her moral compass true.

Which was a good thing considering that Watchers, as direct descendants of fallen angels, were born with the power to hold the fabric of the Universe together—or tear it apart. Young Watchers had to be trained to use that magic, and each had different strengths and abilities with it. If Jess was too young and untrained to manifest that yet, it was only a matter of time before she did so on her own. Or before circumstances forced the question.

Last but not least came Corey, with her fire-engine red bob and painted black fingernails. She wore black-and-white skull cameos in her ears, around her neck, and on her fingers. Her polished white halo reminded me of bones—her magic allowed her to speak with the dead, which had been instrumental in saving all our skins.

Corey moved to stand beside Faith. The way she leaned toward

Faith seemed protective. That wasn't entirely new. The group took care of one another, and they'd done more than contemplate how to keep Faith safe from me if need be—if the Angel managed to take me over and I lost control. What felt new was Corey taking point on that rather than Ben, who'd always done so before.

I explained the situation to them as clearly as I could. No one else took it as nonchalantly as Faith had.

Ben folded his arms across his chest. Disbelief tinged his deep voice. "You're not actually going to go looking for your mentor, are you? That'd be like handing yourself over to the Order. Or walking into a trap."

"It's one hundred percent a trap," Jess said.

"Yep," I said. "One that's already set and closed around us. I don't think there's a way out of it."

Corey blinked at me. "What—they have us surrounded?"

"They wouldn't have made themselves known without covering all their bases first."

"What now?" Faith asked.

"The only way out is through," I said.

Red met my gaze. "Play the game better than they do."

I nodded. "Any of you drive over here?"

"Me," Corey said.

Unlike Red's truck, her car would hold five people. "Addie's expecting all of you. Red will drive you over in Corey's car, and you'll stay there until you hear from the rest of us."

She didn't ask why Red had to do the driving. The answer was obvious: in case of trouble.

Ben poured on a little sarcasm. "What do we do if the Order kills you and dumps your body in the Willamette?"

"Whatever Red and Addie tell you," I said.

I glanced at Red. "Take them out the front door and walk to the car. Stay close to each other. Ben, can you shield the car once Red pulls into traffic?"

"Definitely," he said.

That should conceal them from magical vision and any magic the

Order might throw at them. It wouldn't cover electronic surveillance or a good old-fashioned tail. Then again, the Order would've staked out Addie's house, along with my apartment and Red's place.

"Just watch yourselves," I said.

The kids trudged back up the stairs—all except Faith. She met my gaze with her gold-streaked eyes, and suddenly I saw only her, not the god.

"This is different than anything we've done before," she said.

I nodded.

She swallowed hard. "Please promise me that you'll come back."

I'd spent almost all the time I'd known her lying to her. About how I'd come to find her. About who I'd been. About why I'd saved her life. I'd promised myself I'd never lie to her again. It had to be the truth, and only the truth, or else how could she ever trust me again?

It came down to one thing: I was her rock.

She could count on the others. They were her friends. They'd do anything to help her, to protect her—even if it meant finding a safe house and keeping it secret from me so they'd have a place to go to ground if there were ever an altercation between the Angel inside of me and the Awakened inside Faith. Which her friends had actually done. Thinking about it still left me gobsmacked.

They were good friends. The best, in fact, and I was grateful that Faith had them.

She hadn't known them as long as she had me, however. I was the touchstone, the bridge from her innocence to where she stood now.

I called her my daughter, and she accepted it even though I wasn't her birth mother, and "adopted mother" didn't suit either. Even so, I was the closest and only thing she had to a mother. I'd die for her.

"I'll try," I said.

She held my gaze for long minute, then nodded.

"Okay." She wiped her palms on the front of her leggings, then turned and followed her friends.

I took a shaky breath and blew it out slowly.

Unless I'd read things all wrong, the initial level of risk was relatively low. Sunday, Miguel, and I would find out what Lily wanted and we'd go from there. I didn't expect it to be simple. I didn't expect it to be safe.

Red closed the distance between us. "I can see what's happening in your brain. Gears turning."

Faith wasn't the only one who needed me to come back, and come back whole and well. After the conversation Red and I had in his office before Lily had shown up, things between us felt clearer, and at the same time more vulnerable, more tender.

Love was no small thing. It was everything.

"You can't read my mind," I said.

"You're thinking there's too many considerations for us to handle. The kids and me, we're not professionals. What if the Order decides to do something we can't counter? What if they kill us and dump *our* bodies in the Willamette?"

I wanted to tell him that if that came to pass, I'd kill Lily with prejudice and bloody as much of the Order as I could before someone managed to take me down. I'd mean it, too.

He knew all that, and he didn't relish the thought.

I sighed. "Just be careful."

"Careful as I can," he said.

He cupped his hand against the nape of my neck and pulled me close. I slipped my hands inside his coat and wrapped my arms around him. He kissed me on the mouth and then in the center of my forehead, breathing me in.

I did the same, drawing in the scent of grass and earth, tasting the lingering sweetness of his mouth. I held him as tightly as I could, molding my body to his, letting him know that as much as he was here for me, I was here for him.

After a moment, I loosened my grip, and he drew back.

His eyes crinkled at the corners. "See you later."

"As soon as I can," I said.

It was the best adult promise I could give him.

He pulled free and followed the kids up the steps. I watched him go, saying a prayer under my breath for safety.

I did it automatically, as if it were something I did all the time. I hadn't prayed since the night my parents had died. I didn't believe in God with a capital G. I believed in people, whether human or fae—even the damn angels. I believed in the world. All the worlds.

Maybe that was who I prayed to. All of us. The better angels of our natures.

I let the last word of prayer leave my lips and float on the air to follow my people, to watch over them.

As they filed out into the hush before dawn, the two people I needed most right now filed in.

ACKNOWLEDGMENTS

This story, like its predecessor, was inspired by Michael Klaas, Miles, Brandon, CJ, Zack, and Claire. Thank you for excellent company and long, action-packed afternoons. To Jo Anne Banker, T. Thorn Coyle, JC Andrijeski, and Danielle Rivera, thank you for reading the draft manuscript and for your always-excellent suggestions.

Special thanks also goes out to the members of Awakened Magic: Aaron, Richard, Kandice, William, Ashley, Rebecca, Paula, Fiona, Nadine, Amber, Jannetta, Kathleen, Brandi, Ron, and Ravyn.

Much love.

ABOUT THE AUTHOR

Since the age of seven, Leslie Claire Walker has wanted to be Princess Leia—wise and brave and never afraid of a fight, no matter the odds.

Leslie hails from the concrete and steel canyons and lush bayous of southeast Texas—a long way from Alderaan. Now, she lives in the rain-drenched Pacific Northwest with a cast of spectacular characters, including cats, harps, fantastic pieces of art that may or may not be doorways to other realms, and too many fantasy novels to count.

She is the author of *The Faery Chronicles* and *Soul Forge* series, two complete series of urban fantasy novels, novellas, and stories filled with found family, angels, assassins, faeries, and demons.

Connect with Leslie
leslieclairewalker.com
leslie@leslieclairewalker.com

9 781960 168030